SPY OR DIE

A SPY, CRIME THRILLER AND ROMANCE NOVEL
WITH
SPIRITUAL CONTENT

Carrie Wachsmann

Heart Beat
PRODUCTIONS INC.

Published by

HeartBeat Productions Inc.
Box 633, Abbotsford, BC, Canada V2T 6Z8
email: info@heartbeat1.com
website: heartbeat1.com
604.852.3761

Cover design and artwork: Carrie Wachsmann
Photo images: Pexels.com free images of women - credits - Cottonbro
Photo images: Pixabay.com free image of dog, aircraft, image of man
Photo image: Woman rock climbing - permission

ISBN 1-895112-76-1
978-1-895112-76-4 (paperback)

Printed in the USA

DEDICATED TO

THOSE WHO RISK THEIR LIVES
TO RESCUE THE CAPTIVES

KEEPING THE ART OF STORYTELLING ALIVE

CONTENTS

AUTHOR'S NOTES

Creating this action-filled, could-very-well-be-true-if-you-are-a-conspiracy-theorist, crime thriller was gratifying.

Spy or Die, has three main themes running through it. They are "forever young," "the God factor" and "human trafficking."

"Forever young." Growing older can be both challenging and great at the same time. Part of it is one's choice. I am discovering. At some point in our growing older, we all come to that place where we have to address that we are no longer 25, or 35, or 45.

And at some point we all come face to face with our mortality - **"the God factor."**

"Human trafficking" - Human suffering is a tragic part of this world. Can we make a difference? Do our choices and the stand we take for truth and integrity make a difference? What can I do, regardless of age, to help ease the suffering of others around me?

After turning 50, wanting to deal with my not-necessarily-accurate perceptions of growing older, (one being at some point you get put on the shelf) I started working on a story that addressed some of my misperceptions.

I had a simple idea for a story, not caring if it would develop into a novel or not. The pressure was off. I was able to have fun with a storyline that captures some of the fears and hopes, challenges and tragedies, impossibilities and victories one can experience during a lifetime.

CHARACTERS

Dani Wells	Kidnapped victim
Jack Wells	Dani's husband
Bentley	Jack's Rottweiler
Jogger, Tom and Gerry	Kidnappers
Jason Whiting (manager)	Starbucks staff
Valentina Jarez	Starbucks staff
Mora	Hair stylist
Suit #1 and Suit #2	Kidnappers & enforcers
Rev. Graham Smith	Jack's long time friend
Betty	Church secretary and receptionist
2 officers	Deliver the news of abduction
Officer Faro	At the precinct taking statements
Donna	Female officer – Dani's friend
Lance Copper	Police Chief/close friend of Jack's
Conner, Miller and Staner	Special Agents on the case
Heather Benson	Reported the speeding van
Her son Jimmy	Playing soccer in the back alley
Brandon	Playing soccer in the back alley
Gregory	Plane attendant
Jody	Plane attendant
Unnamed	Plane attendant
Dr. Pitt	Dr. on the plane
Abducted women	Jane Russell #6 (AKA Dani) Kelly #1, Marcie #2, Becky #3, Gracie #4, Sandra #5
Dr. Frankel	Scientist, program designer/enforcer
Clay, Mack, Billy, Pete, Cam and J.D.	6 Mercenaries – Served with Jack
John Madson	Sgt Major project fighter trainer
Bacardi	Evil billionaire technologist Head of project Spy or Die at headquarters
TurnKey Intelligence	Headquarters
Will Bradson	Injured security guard left behind

SETTING THE STAGE

It's February 2002—the suburbs of Seattle, WA USA. Dani and her husband, Jack, are living the good life. That is about to change.

Notes: About tracking devices and their origin.
According to Wikipedia, the inventor of the GPS device is unknown. *"Well up to my knowledge finding the inventor of GPS device is a very tough thing... it's a debatable topic... the inventor of GPS device, whoever she/he maybe is lying in the dark side of history.*
https://www.quora.com/Who-invented-the-GPS-tracking-device

About the law and Human Trafficking.
*"In 2000 the United Nations adopted the Protocol to Prevent, Suppress and Punish Trafficking in Persons Especially Women and Children. Often referred to as the **Palermo Protocol**. Since then, more than 150 countries have signed on to this Protocol against Human Trafficking, committing them to preventing, protecting and prosecuting violators of the Protocol. Of these countries, 140 have made Human Trafficking a criminal offence.

Countries that have signed on to the **Palermo Protocol** agree that Human Trafficking is a serious crime and violation of human rights. The Protocol provides an internationally accepted definition of 'trafficking in persons,' containing three parts."*

Action: *'the recruitment, transportation, transfer, harboring or receipt of persons.'*

Means: *'by any means of threat or use of force or other forms of coercion, of abduction, of fraud, of deception, of the abuse of power or of a position of vulnerability or of giving or receiving of payments or benefits to achieve the consent of a person having control over another person.'*

Purpose: *'for the purpose of exploitation. Exploitation shall include at a minimum the exploitation of the prostitution of others or other forms of sexual exploitation, forced labor or services, slavery of practices similar to slavery, servitude or the removal of organs…'"*

For more detailed information: https://owjn.org/2018/06/the-law-and-human-trafficking-in-canada/ (The Law and Human Trafficking in Canada website)

SCENE 1

DANI

February 7th, 2002

Dani Wells stands in front of a full-length bedroom mirror and exhales audibly. Today is her 50th birthday. She has determined not to let this milestone affect her negatively in any way, and yet lately, she has become noticeably introspective.

Having slipped on a pair of dark green Alan Mills Expedition pants and camisole, Dani stepped back, slid her hips to the side, straightened her shoulders and gave herself a critical twice over. A slight smile crossed her face as she touched the scar that ran across her cheek. She had grown to like her scar. It was part of her, her survival story.

For a fifty-year-old, she was in remarkable shape, even youthful-looking. *Well,* she mused, *I've worked hard to keep in shape.* She had to admit it took determination and self-control, but for Dani, it was well worth the efforts.

She had noticed the tiny lines creeping around her deep-blue eyes, but for the most part, she was still able to hide them. Being more of a purist than not, she relied on natural remedies to fight the battle of ageing. Something her grandmother had taught her.

"Nature has a way of meeting our needs and granting our wishes, if we only give her a chance," she always said.

Dani flipped back her rich, dark-brown shoulder-length hair. *I'd better pick up another box of Herbalcare hair color this week. Those tiresome roots are beginning to show, and unfortunately, grandma's advice doesn't apply to hair color.* She bent forward and looked intently at herself in the mirror.

Then again, maybe it's time to do something different. Yes, I think it is time. I'm going to make an appointment with a stylist, is what I'm going to do. Today she liked that thought. Today she would be impulsive. *If I plan it, I can be impulsive—yes, I can—what better time than now? I've been thinking about this long enough.*

Dani grabbed her appointment book and looked through her contacts until she reached "Mora, hairstylist." She met Mora several months ago at a local Women's Trade Show. Dani stopped to watch one of Mora's on-stage makeover sessions and was impressed with both the woman and her skills. She decided if the time came to do something drastically different with her hair, she'd call Mora.

She made the call. "Good morning, my name is Dani. I would like to make an appointment with Mora for early this afternoon if possible. I know the chance of getting an appointment at such short notice is probably slim to none, but I thought I'd give it a try before I change my mind, if you know what I mean. It's been a long time since I let anyone touch my hair."

The voice on the other end was pleasant and cheerful. "Good morning, Dani. What are you looking to have done today?"

"A makeover pretty much. I've got long dark hair and I want to walk out of your salon an ice platinum blond with perhaps a smidgen of dark undertones. I know, that might be asking a lot."

"Well it will take a few hours and Mora books a week in advance, but let me take a look. What do you know, you are in luck. She had a cancellation for 10:45. If that works for you, I can book you in."

"Excellent. I'll make it work. Thanks."

Dani dropped her phone into her handbag. She slipped into a white, fitted cotton shirt with open collar and raced down the stairs. *Dear Jack. He booked off the morning to make me breakfast.*

Jack smiled and gave her an admiring glance as he poured a glass of fresh-squeezed orange juice. Still holding the pitcher in one hand and the glass in the other, Jack reached out for a kiss. "Happy birthday, my sweet."

Dani wrapped her arms around him. A contented, "Umm," was her response.

Bentley, Jack's retired pure-bred Rottweiler police K9, dosing on his personal, once strictly-forbidden leather two-seater, yawned. Not wanting to miss out on some early morning affection, he stretched and clumsily made his way towards Jack and Dani. His rear-end wiggled back and forth in cheerful greeting.

"Good morning to you too, Bentley," Dani said. Bentley nudged Dani's hand, returning the greeting, then lay down on her feet with a thump.

Bentley had retired early after being wounded in service. He took a bullet to the chest, one meant for Jack, and lived to bark about it. The scar on his side was a glaring reminder.

"Your choice," Jack offered, "Blueberry crepes with whipped cream or—a Spanish omelet with all the trimmings. Which will it be?"

saying goes, the rest is history.

In an instant, the special agent (CID – Criminal Investigation Division, US Marine Corps) who strode into the laboratory that day turned Dani's fascinating project into more of a thriller. As the

for the advancement of medical science.)

Jack was investigating the mysterious disappearance of a deceased Lance Corporal. Dani worked as a journalist, reporting on the pros and cons of becoming a "whole-body donor." (Donating one's body

places—standing over a cadaver!

Dani and Jack had married late in life; she was thirty-eight, and he, forty-three. Two free-spirited individuals, who love adventure and don't have a great deal of patience with the confines of society's unnecessary rigid rules, found each other in the most unlikely of

knew.

Maybe that's why she needed to stay in shape, why getting older was beginning to be painful. Maybe she was afraid one day if she didn't keep up with him, she would lose him. A silly thought, she

sick.

"Good choice." As far as her man Jack goes in Dani's eyes, there wasn't a lot he couldn't do. He was pretty much perfect as far as she was concerned. Not only was he the most ruggedly handsome man she had ever laid eyes on, he was also strong and muscular, athletic, dark-haired with splashes of gray, always tanned, and never

"I think I'll have the same."

She asked.

Dani sat on the stool by the counter and watched as Jack whipped up her birthday breakfast request. "And you, what will you have?"

"We can do that."

"I'll take the blueberry crepes with Greek yogurt?"

Jack and Dani do not have children, not by choice, a fact that carries a bit of a sting for them both. There isn't much about Jack that Dani doesn't like. He's not excited about gardening and yard work, is a restless sleeper, and when he's upset about something, he will leave for hours. This disappearing act doesn't happen often, so Dani doesn't have much about which to complain.

Suddenly a wave of regret swept over Dani. For months now, she had been too busy for the two of them to spend much quality time together. *I've been neglecting the one person in my life that means the most to me! Not good. Seems like I've been neglecting a lot of things.*

"I've been neglecting you," she blurted out. "I want to do more of this." She spoke wistfully, her voice showing her regret.

Jack looked up. "I wouldn't say neglecting. I like that part about spending more time, but what about your research assignment?"

"Well, I'm going to talk to my boss and tell him we'll have to get an extension."

"Really, when did you decide this?"

"Now."

"Now? That isn't at all like you. What happened?"

"I think maybe it's got to do with time creeping up on me, or something like that. Lately, I've been thinking about what's important to me. It's not that this assignment isn't important or that I don't enjoy it. I love it. It's just that I shouldn't have to sacrifice my time with you."

"It's not all your fault. Sometimes my work takes me away for two weeks or more." Jack carefully slid the blueberry crepe onto her plate, added some fresh blueberries, a scoop of Greek yogurt, and placed it in front of the love of his life.

He reached under the counter and handed Dani several sprays of exquisite purple, white and green orchids.

"Ooh! Now those are perfect! — my favorite. Thank yooouu."

"Classy flowers for one classy lady."

"I absolutely love them, and I do love you, Jack." Dani pulled herself up and reached over the counter to kiss Jack. This time they lingered.

"I should be home by 5:00 today," she whispered.

"How about I take you out to dinner, and we can spend the evening together," Jack suggested.

"Now there's a thought. I'll be here."

"Then it's a date."

SCENE 2

THE SUSPICIOUS DIRTY WHITE VAN

 **A** dirty, white delivery van with tinted windows and two occupants, is parked across the street in full view of Starbucks window, Main Street and Nelson Avenue. A jogger in black sweats and dark-blue hoody, wearing sunglasses, stops next to the van's passenger window, stretches, and takes several deep breaths. The window rolls down a few inches.

"Starbucks window, far left. Long dark hair. Brown ¾ length jacket." The jogger speaks so only those in the vehicle can hear.

The driver, wearing a grease-smudged orange cap, raises a pair of binoculars to his eyes and peers across the street towards the popular coffee house.

He lowers the binoculars and nods. The jogger continues his run. The driver is Gerry. Mid-sized and in his thirties, he looks intelligent. "Soon as she leaves the building, we roll," he says to his partner in the passenger's seat.

SCENE 3

THE APPOINTMENT AT STARBUCKS

Dani races her sporty, bright blue Audi R9 into the Starbucks parking lot just a little too fast and parks, taking up two spots. She has an appointment in precisely three minutes with someone she believes has essential information regarding her research project. She grabs her bag and rushes into the shop.

Dani noted the woman sitting in her favorite spot by the window on the sunny side, far right corner. She watched the woman drain her cup. *Good, looks like she'll be leaving soon.* Dani glanced around and, not seeing her interviewee, took a deep breath and relaxed.

"I'll have coffee-mocha, no whipped cream—wait, it's my birthday, I'll take the whipped cream."

"Well, happy birthday, Dani." The server smiled. His almost too-perfect white teeth complimented his frosted-tipped, mused-up Faux Hawk hairstyle.

He was somewhere in his early thirties but looked more like twenty-oneish. "Since you're one of my favorite customers, and it's your birthday, the coffee-mocha with whipped cream is on me."

"Oh, I didn't mean for you…"

"Of course you didn't. You're looking drop-dead gorgeous today, by the way. So—thirty-nine???"

"Now you know you can't be flirting with me, Jason. How many times do I have to remind you I am very happily married."

"I know, I know. Just kiddin'. I'd never date a married woman; you know that. But if you weren't married…"

Dani smiled and took her drink. "Jason, once you decide to settle down and pick one woman, you'll find her, and she will be a lucky lady."

"You think so?"

"I know so."

The steam machine whirled its song as Jason automatically prepared Dani's coffee-mocha, her way. A tanned, striking young woman with strong Hispanic features returned from wiping tables and began taking orders. *She must be new.* Dani noticed her flawless skin, her perfect, small hands and long graceful fingers, her athletic, shapely figure. Hair tied back; she was not wearing makeup. *No need for makeup. Now there's a woman for Jason.*

"So, how old are you?" Jason continued.

"Jason, the first thing you are going to have to learn is that you never ask a woman her age?"

"You don't?"

"You don't, but then I'm sure you've heard that before." Dani paused. She couldn't help noticing the woman, now watching Jason, listening intently to their conversation. "Valentina," her name tag read.

Jason, oblivious to anyone else but Dani, boldly held her gaze, hopeful she would give in.

Dani smiled, and to her surprise, she said, almost proudly, "Today I am fifty." *Seriously, being fifty is getting easier by the hour!*

Jason sputtered. "You're joshing me! Na, you are joshing me."

Dani shrugged her shoulders and turned to see if the woman sitting in her favorite window seat had left—the woman was just getting up to leave. Always observant, Dani noted the woman wore her hair very similar to herself; same color, same style; she even had strikingly similar features! To Dani's disapproval, she noted the woman was also wearing a ¾ length jacket much like the one she was wearing; same color, style, but unlike Dani's, this woman's jacket was noticeably weathered, with frayed sleeves and hemline. Dani's disapproval quickly turned to sympathy as the woman brushed past her. *Not a happy person, that one. She looks tired and worn out.* In an instant, Dani's disapproval changed to remorse. Remorse for passing judgment on someone about whom she knew nothing and for something as trivial as "similarities." If she had more time, she would find a way to strike up a conversation—but today was not that day.

As Dani slid into the sunny booth, a strange, unexplainable feeling swept over her. Her life had been too smooth, too perfect, other than, of course, too busy. She hadn't valued her good fortune or treasured it nearly enough. That woman could have been her. *I have taken my good life for granted.* At that moment, Dani determined, *that's gotta change. No idea how, but it's gotta change.*

Dani looked at her watch. *Mr. Langdon, where are you? You are late.* Was her cell phone turned on? Of course it was. She always had her cell phone turned on. Just in case, she rifled through her bag and dug out her phone. Yes, it was on, and the volume was on high. Mr. Langdon was now twelve minutes late.

Her phone rang. This would be him calling to let her know he was driving into the parking lot. "Hello."

"Hi, it's me. I was thinking. Why don't we go for a drive up to Crystal Mountain, take the sky-lift and have dinner with a view? What do you say?"

"Jack, I would love that. I have to…"

"Is that a yes?"

Dani hesitated, thinking about the hair appointment. "I've got a few things to do first. The earliest I can be home is 3:00."

"That works. I'll make the reservation. See you then."

"OK, see you then."

Her client was now fifteen minutes late. Not good. She'd give him twenty minutes, and if he hadn't arrived by then, well, she would try to rebook. It had taken her several weeks to get Mr. Langdon to agree to a meeting. As an Adams, Adams and Gray Legal Researcher, she was gathering pertinent information for a class-action lawsuit involving the waste management company where Mr. Langdon was an employee.

(ring)

"Hello."

"Hello, Dani Wells?" the voice said.

"Yes, this is Dani Wells."

"This is Mr. Langdon's assistant. He asked me to call you. He is very sorry. He is being held up in an urgent matter and is unable to meet with you today.

Alternatively, he is available Thursday at 8:00 AM if that suits you."

"Let me check my schedule. One moment please."

Good, he wants to rebook. Dani dug out her little black appointment book. She flipped through it. *Yes. Thursday morning is open.* "That would be fine, thank you. Thursday 8:00 AM it is. The same place." Dani slipped the phone into her inside jacket pocket. She closed her eyes and, wrapping her fingers around the warm paper cup, slowly sipped its hot, creamy contents. *I've plenty of time so relax girl and enjoy your coffee mocha.*

SCENE 4

THE ABDUCTION

The dirty, white van with its two occupants is still parked directly across the street. Windows tinted, the occupant's actions go unnoticed by passers-by. The driver raises a pair of binoculars to his eyes for the umpteenth time and peers across the street towards the popular coffee house.

"This is taking a mite longer than expected," he muttered. "It looks like she's finishing up now. She's draining her cup." He continued to give an account of the moves the woman in the window was making; more it seemed to himself than his partner. "Soon as she moves to go, we travel."

"Got a light?" asked his partner.

"What? You moron. Put that away. Do you know what we're doing here?" The driver didn't expect an answer. "#!%$, a delivery truck right in my #%&!' view!" "Move, move, MOVE." The driver slammed his open hand onto the steering wheel. "Tom, get out and do something. Post her position. Now! Move man. We've got to keep her in our sights."

Tom came to attention. He wasn't the brighter of the two, but by the looks of him, he could have moved the van on his strength alone. He opened the van door, stepped out, and casually stepped towards the newspaper stand a few feet in front of them. Taking his time, he went through his pockets, looking for loose change. Not able to see the window across the street, he moved ahead a few more paces.

Traffic suddenly became congested and commercial vehicles lined the street, blocking his view. Then the delivery truck pulled out into the street, and things started to move again. Tom casually made his way back to the van.

"She's right where we left her, Gerry, buddy," Tom said. "We still got her in our sights."

Gerry didn't answer, his attention focused entirely on the subject. He noticed the "subject" was sipping her drink again. "What? I thought she finished that java already."

"Whaddya say?" Tom asked.

"Nothin'. Nothin'."

Silence once again in the van. Gerry reached for his cigarettes, then hesitated, his hand hovered over the box. He pulled his hand back and placed it back on the steering wheel.

Tom chuckled. "I know, it's tempting, isn't it?"

Gerry ignored Tom. Twenty-three minutes passed. Then Gerry reached for the key and turned on the ignition. "Looks like she's leaving. OK, OK, she's leaving for real this time."

The two men watched as the woman took her last sip, grabbed her bag, and slid out of the booth. Gerry turned the key, put the van into gear, and moving with the traffic, slipped into the lane, and seeing a break in the traffic, made a sharp left turn into the Starbucks parking lot.

Dani fished in her purse for her keys as she meandered to her car. *Today is going to be the best day ever, and it's about time.*

Tom flung open the van side-door and jumped out, landing beside Dani. Momentarily stunned, Dani froze. The intent of her attacker—obvious—a black balaclava covered his face. There was no mistaking; she was the target, and yet her mind refused to accept it. *This can't be real. What is going on? I have a hair appointment, and besides, it's my birthday. My keys—where are my keys? Where are the guy's hands? Does he have a weapon?*

A myriad of thoughts scrambled through Dani's brain. *It's true*, her brain screamed. *Everything feels like slow motion. I can't seem to move.*

Now, all this lasted less than three seconds, and Dani knew three seconds was the maximum she had before she would have to snap into action if she was going to have a chance against her attacker. Being the wife of an Ex-Navy Seal, her self-defence strategies were deeply ingrained. She just hadn't expected to need it today.

Then the man stepped into her space and reached out his hand to grab her. That is when Dani snapped into action. She reacted as she had trained. She side-stepped to the left, grasped her attacker's arm, locking his elbow as she pinned it to herself. Meanwhile, her free hand slammed like a knife into his throat. Instinctively, a knee went to the groin. All in one smooth move, her attacker buckled to his knees, in excruciating pain, gasping for breath.

A prayer rushed to Dani's lips. "Oh God, help. Help me," she cried.

Her bag, where was her bag? She had dropped it, and during the scuffle, the big man had kicked it. Where was it? She had to forget about her bag. *Where are those keys?*

Dani's attacker was picking himself up now, slowly, holding his throat, still making rasping sounds. The man in the driver's seat was yelling at her attacker. Something about being an idiot, and he had one job to do…

My keys. She needed her keys. There, she spotted them under her attacker's vehicle. *There's no way I can get to those keys.* Dani noted, the second man was stepping out of the van. She also noted he had something in his hand. Peripherally, Dani could see that the first guy was back on his feet, staggering towards her. She didn't wait this time. She moved in with a swift kick to the side of the knee.

The second attacker rushed in, grabbing Dani around the neck. Instinctively she grabbed the arm twice the size of hers with one hand and slipped her body to the side, giving herself that fraction of an inch for breathing room. She brought her elbow straight up, strong, bone meeting chin. The man's head snapped backward. Dani reached for his face. Her well-manicured fingernails went directly to his right eye. She ripped off his balaclava, exposing his face to the world.

Please, somebody, remember that face. Her fingers dug grooves into his leathered skin as they made their way back to his eye. The man roared, a roar filled with pain and anger. A rag that smelled strong and putrid was smothering her now. Dani struggled, and with a fierceness she did not know she possessed, dug her fingers deeper into her attacker's eye. Dani melted to the ground like a limp rag doll as the drug took effect. For that split second, that second she would always remember, she watched as her world went black.

Jason was making a Nutella Frappuccino when he heard the yelling, the screams. He dropped the silver pitcher and ran to the window. In horror, he watched a face-covered man grab Dani from behind and wrap his arm around her neck. He saw a second man wincing in pain as he jumped on one leg towards a rust-riddled, dirty white panel van. Dani was fighting for her life!

"911," Jason yelled. He turned and shouted to Valentina, "911, call the police! Dani. She's being attacked. Quick. I'm going after her."

The man's balaclava was now on the ground. Blood covered one side of his face!

Jason grabbed a chair and ran out into the parking lot. "Let her go, leave her alone. Stop, stop," he cried. But by this time, the two had dragged and shoved Dani into the back of the vehicle. Fearlessly Jason ran towards them, the chair raised above his head. He reached the van just in time to smash it into the closing side door. With all his might, he swung the chair again, this time hurling at the driver's window. The window shattered, and so did the chair. With tires squealing, the van fishtailed out onto the back street and quickly disappeared. "MSL 476. Muscle 4 76," Jason muttered under his breath. "Muscle 4 76."

Jason stood alone in the parking lot, both hands resting on the top of his head. He expressed both defeat and dismay. At some point, he dropped his arms to his side, walked in a circle, and returned directly back to where he had been. He put his hands back on his head and stared in the direction where he last saw the van.

Valentina and others began to make their way out onto the parking lot. Valentina went over to Dani's bag, was about to gather up the scattered items and put them back into the bag when she thought better of it. *You know better than to tamper with evidence.* She walked over to Jason. They stood together, looking into the traffic, Jason with his hands still on his head, Valentina beside him.

"911?"

"On their way."

Patrons and bystanders began to gather. That is when the police cars, sirens blaring, surrounded them.

SCENE 5

THE SWITCH

Several street kids having a good time playing soccer in a back alley are unaware of a white van racing towards them. A quiet alley in the warehouse district of Seattle's Lower Durmish River area, this back street does not see much traffic, except for the locals. The driver of the van does not slow down for the soccer game.

"Hey! Look out!" the tallest of the seven yelled. The kids scrambled to get out of harm's way, jumping the neighbor's broken-down picket fence. Several of the frightened youngsters shouted at the driver, cursing him and his vehicle and his relations. A woman, slim, mid-thirties, her long black hair pulled into a ponytail, threw open the back door of her bungalow and raced towards to alleyway, making wild gestures and yelling at the top of her voice, "What do you think you are doing? You scumbag idiots!"

The vehicle barreled ahead, dodging the potholes like some drunk after a night out on the town, travelling towards a row of warehouses several blocks up the road. The kids and the woman watched as the van turned onto Wharf Street and out of sight. They did not see it approach one of the waterfront warehouses, where a commercial-sized metal door, creaking and groaning, slowly rolled up. The van disappeared into a black hole. The door rolled closed behind it.

After a few words and gestures between the kids and the woman, the vexed soccer players "shook it off" and went back to their game. The vexed woman retreated into her house.

Inside the warehouse, two men in black suits removed their unconscious cargo and transported Dani into a black limousine. One of the men slid into the limo beside her, propping her upright as he strapped her into the seatbelt.

"She did all that?" the suit, the one wearing a chauffeur's hat with a smirk on his face, asked. The man looked down at Tom's leg and then turned to look at Gerry; his eye, gashed and swollen shut, dark red blood still streaked heavily across his face.

Gerry shrugged. "How were we to know? All the rest have been a piece of cake. 'cept for one Gracie gangster type …person. She was a bit of trouble, but not like this one."

"Yeah," Tom added. "We were told these were a bunch of worn-out middle-aged skirts. What's with this good-looking, martial arts babe anyway?"

Tom grabbed a broom resting against the wall, turned it upside down, stuck it under his armpit and leaned heavily on it. He let out a groan.

"She doesn't fit the profile, man. You sure you got the right one?" Gerry inquired.

Moving close to Gerry, the one with the chauffeur's hat, no longer wearing a smirk, stuck his face a few inches from Gerry's and replied, "You mean, are YOU sure you got the right one?"

Gerry flinched ever so slightly but held his ground. He didn't reply.

"Course we got the right one," Tom interjected. "We done our job good, didn't we, Gerry. Your guy pointed her out.

"We watched her the whole time and didn't miss a thing, right Gerry."

Gerry and the man ignored Tom. After a pause, the man stepped back, reached into his inside front jacket pocket, and handed Gerry an envelope. Gerry took it, opened it, and counted the thick wad of bills before stuffing them back into the envelope and inside his jacket pocket. Without further conversation, the driver took his place behind the wheel. Tom and Gerry watched as the warehouse door rolled open and the limo left the building.

SCENE 6

THE PROGRAM & BAD NEWS

Jack Wells and Reverend Graham Smith are deep in conversation in the pastor's office. Sitting at a round table, they examine papers with ideas for a youth training program called "Adventures & Attitudes Boot Camp."

Bentley, dead to the world, is lying peacefully at his master's feet. With each breath, he lets out a soft lip-flapping snore. Ever-so-often his muscular body quivers, followed by a gentle whine and back to his gentle snores.

"We've been getting requests lately to lower the age requirements," Jack said. "I don't feel comfortable opening this program up to any young man under the age of 16. And we've got plenty of requests to start up a women's program as well."

Graham nodded. "You've developed quite the challenging program for these youth." He paused. "It's a huge success. I agree. If we were to address the 12 - 15 age group, we would need to make it specific. Right now, the 16 - 19-year-old range is working even better than expected. From our stats, only 22 percent attrition. We're making a difference."

"That we are. There's so much need out there, and we don't have enough quality programs for these at-risk troubled teens."

"Jack, I've been thinking, we need to get serious about that rescue recovery program for girls and women. So many innocent lives lost, day after day, year after year, to the horrors of human trafficking. In our city alone… well, you know my heart. I think it's time we put some plans to the program we've talked about getting off the ground for, what? Five years now?

"At least," Jack answered. "And I've been thinking about that too lately. Last night I woke up with that very thought. You think God might be trying to get our attention? It's way beyond our ability to put together, but certainly not impossible for God."

"And we need to keep that in mind. We need to get that boat into the water and give Him something to work with."

"We're talking about doing rescue missions. We're entering some seriously dangerous territory. I say we think about this for a few days. We're going to need to put together a team, and if God's got in mind for us to pursue this now, He'll let us know who's on the team."

"By the way, I have someone in mind to head up the women's rescue recovery program," the reverend interjected.

"You do? Who might that be?"

"Dani keeps coming to mind. She'd be perfect."

Jack smiled. "She would, wouldn't she. Thing is she's deeply wrapped up in her projects. Not sure what it would take for her to let go of all that. She's a game-changer, and she's exceptional at what she does. Adam, Adams and Gray will not let her go easily. But if it's meant to be, nothing would surprise me."

"You are right. If it's meant to be, it will be."

"I would love it if Dani took up that challenge."

Graham nodded. "I hear you. First things first." The pastor redirected the topic, "Since you joined our team, Jack, we have had some major positive effects on the willing participants, sometimes even on the unwilling. Your military background, combined with your love for God and these youth - I can't express my gratitude and admiration."

Jack smiled. "Thanks, my friend. But, this wouldn't be nearly as successful as it is without you. Who would have thought, one day, you and I, two old school buddies, would be doing this sort of thing together."

"Right. Me a pastor, you an ex-Navy Seal. You could be doing a lot of other things right now."

"This is where I want to be, Graham. After Bosnia and PTS (post-traumatic stress) you helped me get my life back on track. Now it's my turn. I want to do this. I have never felt so satisfied with life."

Someone knocked at the door and Bentley scrambled to his feet. Betty, the church secretary, opened the door and blurted, "There are two police officers at the front desk. They're looking for Jack."

Jack glanced at Graham. "Dani," he whispered. *Something's not right. I hope it's nothing.* His heart told him otherwise as the beats picked up speed.

Without further conversation, Graham and Jack, with the now-very-much-alert Bentley at his heel, followed Betty to the front office.

"Lieut. Colonel Jackery Wells?" the senior of the two officers queried.

"Yes, sirs. What seems to be the problem?"

"Well, sir, we have some difficult news for you. It regards your wife, Danielle." He paused.

Jack glanced at his friend and then replied, "Go on."

"It appears that your wife has been, um, abducted, sir. She was last seen leaving the Starbucks coffee shop at Main and Nelson. Several patrons, witnesses, saw her try to fight off two assailants while still in the parking lot. We do have a description and a license number. I'm sorry, sir."

Graham placed a supportive hand on Jack's shoulder.

Jack's body shuddered as he took his next breath. *Why would anyone want to abduct Dani? This doesn't make sense.*

"Sir, we will need you to come to the station." The officer's voice disrupted Jack's troubled thoughts.

"I'll drive," Graham offered.

Jack nodded. His emotions threatened to engulf him—panic rushed to take over. If ever he needed a supportive and understanding friend, it was now.

Not much could faze Jack, but Dani—Dani— she was his weak spot.

SCENE 7

THE SEARCH BEGINS

Jack, Graham and several police officers sit around the station's boardroom table discussing the details of Dani's abduction. Bentley, still on high alert, sits close to his master, attentive to every word and movement.

Jack did not take long to harness his explosion of emotions and put on his military hat. By the time they arrived at the station, he had his wits about him.

"Give me everything you've got so far," Jack stated.

"Sir, we found this at the scene." Officer Faro handed Jack Dani's handbag. "Dani dropped this in the scuffle. As for the vehicle, it was reported stolen sometime early this morning. The owner, Steven Madley, reported the theft at 8:34 AM and had a friend pick him up for work. He works on the MJM construction site, Marshall Rd., and ..."

"I know the site," Jack interrupted. "Did this Mr. Madley leave the work site at any time after 8:34 AM?"

"No, sir, he did not leave the site."

"Figures," Jack mumbled. He held the bag that contained the black leather handbag. Bentley stuck his nose under Jack's arm and sniffed the bag. He let out a gentle whine. The items contained in Dani's purse were now zip locked, marked, and on the table in front of him. Jack examined them carefully. Item #6—he picked up the bag containing a ripped-out-of-a-magazine photo of the woman with long, ice-blond hair. He spent a little extra time mulling over it. *I saw this on Dani's bedroom dresser just yesterday. Wonder what that's all about.* Jack put it back with the rest of the displayed items.

"For the record, Jack, please confirm, is this your wife's bag? Most of the contents were scattered all over the parking lot, along with her identification, so we need to confirm this is her bag and these are her belongings."

"Affirmative. These appear to be Dani's belongings. Her wallet, her keys, her ID. The lipstick, that's her favorite shade; those are her earrings and the nail clippers with the beaded gecko; those are definitely hers. This magazine clipping, that's hers. The pack of Kleenex —— probably— and these tea bags belong to her—she always carries a few herbal tea bags with her. The dental floss, tape measure, flip mirror—most likely hers, but you'd have to fingerprint them to be sure. This means she won't have any ID on her, will she?" Speaking the obvious, an answer was not expected nor given.

"The balaclava your wife ripped off one of her attackers is in forensics. We should get DNA off of that."

"Good. What's the report on the surveillance video?" Jack asked.

"Yes. About that. Unfortunately, for some reason, the cameras stopped recording at 3:24 AM.

"So we need to assume this was professionally executed as well as premeditated."

"We believe so, sir. Although it's a bit of an anomaly at the moment, it appears to be professionally executed on one hand, but on the other hand, some things simply don't fall into that category.

"Most likely to throw us off the trail. We're still working our way through all this—taking all possible scenarios into consideration."

"But how did they know Dani would be at the coffee shop that morning? Other than the person she was meeting, and probably his or her secretary. She would know if she was being followed, and I haven't noticed any unusual vehicles in our area."

"A question we intend to find the answer to. We'll have those details soon."

"You said there were witnesses. Who are they?" Jack inquired.

"Starbucks manager, Jason Whiting. He's our main witness. Another staff, Valentina Juarez, she's our other most reliable witness."

"You've ruled them out as suspects?"

"Everyone's a suspect, but so far we do not have any evidence they were involved. We have their cell phones and are checking out all contacts. We also checked for recent calls. They both did not receive or make any calls that morning after starting their shift. We will investigate further and are confident if either of them is in on this, we'll find out soon enough. Several other patrons were also in the coffee shop at the time. We are still getting their statements. As I said, everyone's a suspect for now."

"How about descriptions?"

"Between Jason and Valentina, we have a satisfactory description of one of the attackers. The second perp had his face covered, so we're going by attire, body build, frame, and if this guy is on file, the DNA report will confirm."

"We're also in the process of notifying all medical sites as we speak. We do not know how severe their injuries are. Both men could require medical attention."

Officer Faro paused. "Sir, your wife put up one good, impressive fight."

"I'm sure she did. How did they take her? She's good. They would have had to…"

"We think it's Diethyl ether—a quick-acting drug of some sort, at any rate. A rag was found at the site, and it's at the lab. The attacker dropped it while shoving Dani into the van. Thanks to our Starbucks boy, those scumbags, excuse me, sir, the attackers didn't have time to retrieve it. We should have an answer within the next half hour."

A female officer stepped into the room. She handed Jack a composite drawing of the attacker who lost his balaclava to Dani's quick response.

"Thank you, Donna."

"I'm so sorry, Jack." Donna lost her all-business stoic posture and sputtered, "I don't know what to say. It's all so horrible. Her voice shook along with her hands."

"I know, Donna. I'm having trouble getting my head around all this myself."

"We all love her. You know that, Jack."

"I know. And I am so grateful for that. I have friends—we, Dani and I have good friends here."

Donna pulled herself together. "This man in the composite drawing, he's yet to be identified, but the two witnesses are looking through the files. This could take a while.

"Beatrice in Forensics is running it through our database. Starting with our 'most wanted' list, as well as anyone with a criminal record, especially those recently released. Checking into any possible connections with those recently released and those still doing time, and who might have a past connection with you, Jack."

"Good work."

"Do you know any reason why someone would want to abduct Dani?" Officer Faro interjected. "Anything happen recently that's out of the ordinary?"

"Well, I know it's not for my money. My gut says this is not your regular sort of kidnapping scenario. More likely to be revenge – payback of some sort. I've put a lot of bad guys away. Some died at my hand. Not memories I wish to revisit, but most I don't regret. Put it simply; not everybody likes me."

"Any specific names come to mind?"

"I've got names. I can give you a list and details that might be helpful. Thing is, I haven't had any warning signs. Nothing. No threats, no unusual phone calls, no suspicious vehicles, nothing. And my reticular activator is still working just fine—at least I think it is.

"I know how well your reticular works. You've got eyes behind your head and a sixth sense I'd give plenty for. I've got several detectives ready to set up at your home—we'll wait for a call, just in case this is a kidnapping. Our key witness, Jason, did say that the victim, your wife (looks apologetically at Jack) had been waiting for a client, and he observed her use her cell phone on several occasions while in the coffee shop. We still haven't located her cell. Obviously, it wasn't in her bag. We've got men sweeping the Starbucks area. Maybe it'll show up."

"I know she was working on a rather sensitive project. She was gathering information on a local waste removal company.

"She had a meeting at Starbucks with somebody from the company. She said it was essential to her case. I recall her saying she had been trying to get an interview with this person for some time. They had vital information they were willing to give her. We need to find out who this informant is."

Chief Copper stepped into the room. A look of relief swept over Jack's face.

"Dani works for Adams, Adams and Gray, SEC Lawyers. The waste management company is Clean Waste Removal Enterprises," Jack continued as he stood to greet the chief.

"Jack."

"Chief."

Their handshake went beyond a working relationship, one that indicated a long-term relationship.

"Officer Stanley, officer Courtney, do some digging on this waste removal company, 'Clean Waste Removal Enterprises.'" Chief Copper ordered.

"And Adams Adams and Gray, see what they've got on this waste removal company. Get everything there is to get. If you need help, you've got it. He paused, then added, speaking to Jack, "You think it's our lead?"

"Too simple," Jack answered.

The chief nodded in agreement.

"We still have to follow it."

"Of course. We'll see where it leads. If there is something going on that suggests a cover-up, we'll find it."

"What about Dani's computer?"

"She keeps everything at her office, far as I know. We should double check, though. Search her things at the house. Whatever it takes. We're heading there now." Jack paused. "Any sighting of the van?"

"None," the chief answered. "We do know we're looking for a dirty, beat-up, white delivery van, probably 1988/89 Chevy, smashed driver window, license number MSL 476."

"How so?"

"Witness, Jason Whiting, smashed a chair into the window and memorized the licence number. He's pretty brave as well as observant for a Starbucks guy. He also mentioned your wife talked about a hair appointment. Says he's taking science at the university and needs to support his habit. He has dreams of becoming a forensic scientist. Everything checks out. He gave a very detailed description of our perp. He could be a credible witness."

"A hair appointment, you say? She didn't say anything to me about a hair appointment. But then again, I don't recall her making any hair appointments in months."

The chief nodded understandingly.

"Hold on a minute." Jack reached out and picked up the zip lock bag with the ripped-out-of-a-magazine photo of the woman with the sassy hairstyle. "Something tells me this has to do with her hair appointment."

"Think she was going to surprise you with a new look."

"I think so. We had a birthday dinner date for tonight. It's her fiftieth and she seemed a little out of sorts about the big one."

Bentley nuzzled Jack's hand. "Well, Bentley, You're gonna have to work with us on this one. Like old times— whad ya say, buddy? You've still got your skills. Ready to go into action?" Jack scratched Bentley's ear. Bentley listened intently and answered with a low growl. Then rested his oversized paw up on Jack's arm and let out an eager whine.

"See, you're all business. We've got to find Dani, partner; we got to find her before it's too late."

The war dog was back. Ears perked, eyes bright, Bentley gave a loud, deep bark, raced to the door, and turned to wait for his master.

Jack

SCENE 8

DANI'S NEW REALITY

Dani sits belted, cuffed and bound to an airplane seat, slouched over, head bobbing. In a few minutes, she will realize just how upside down her world is about to become.

As Dani's senses began to waken, she heard a hum; the hum of an engine of sorts! The first thing on her mind, as she started to come to, was how dry her mouth was, and what was that terrible chemical taste? She unsuccessfully tried to move her limp body; her limbs felt rubbery. She felt the cold metal of handcuffs. Her eyes refused to open. She heard several voices.

Disoriented, she told her brain to "wake up" to "think" to "engage." Why was her body behaving so strangely, and why was she handcuffed? Where was she going and with whom?

After several minutes, her eyes began to cooperate, and then slowly, the rest of her body followed. She opened her eyes just long enough to confirm her suspicions she was in an airplane. By the voices, she determined there were at least four people, whom she assumed to be attendants.

Dani noticed a woman unconscious, seated across the aisle.

She observed several more flopping heads stuck out from seats in front of her.

Two attendants started walking in her direction. Dani quickly shut her eyes. *Best let them think I'm still out of it. I need more time to orient myself.* The events of the past few hours were coming back to her in waves. The scene at the Starbuck's parking lot—the two men with balaclavas—the attack—the fight—the big, square face, the smelly rag and then blackness. That's why the terrible taste—the lingering pungent, sweet smell stuck in her nostrils sickened her.

"We've got our packages; all six of them. It appears everything went as planned." *A male*, Dani noted. "We did have one minor glitch, but I don't think that will make any difference now," the voice continued.

The attendants stopped next to Dani. "The Tom and Gerry team messed up on our little Jane Russell here."

Is that me they're talking about? It is me they're talking about!

"Our feisty #6. She was a little more feisty than those two moron cowboy's expected. And we could have witnesses. But 'The Man' said he'd take care of them."

"Doesn't pay to mess up in this business." A woman's voice this time.

"So true. You don't want to even *think* about messing up."

Dani continued to take in all the sounds around her. She drew her attention to the other two persons near the cockpit. She heard the door of the cockpit open, then muffled voices. *More male voices.*

A few seconds later, a woman's voice. Talking in low tones to the other male attendant, Dani assumed the woman was trying not to be heard by the other two attendants whose discussion had moved to other things than "feisty #6."

"So, tell me, Gregory, you're an inside man. What's the 'Spy or Die Project' really about anyway?" The woman whispered.

"Well, Jody, if I tell you, I'd have to kill you," Gregory whispered back.

"Really?" Jody's voice revealed her deep curiosity. She was either very naive or very brave. "You are joking, right? Tell me what you can then. I figure I got a right to know **something**."

"I really can't tell you much. Seriously, that would put you in danger, and you wouldn't want that."

"So, what CAN you tell me?"

"O.K. These women," Gregory pointed, "They're all guinea pigs for some massive 'intervention project,' is what they call it."

"I know that. What kind of project? What kind of intervention are we talking about?"

"It's much bigger than you could ever comprehend. If this project is a success, our entire world will never be the same. In ways, you can't even imagine."

"Whoa!"

"I can also tell you that no one is ever going to miss any of these—these packages. They're either straight off the streets, addicts, some of them homeless, no one loves them, no one who will miss them. Like #3 over there. She's got some jerk for a partner who's a known criminal seems no one can touch, and who's going to kill her eventually anyway. We're doing these women a big favour."

"So, what do they need them for?" Jody exclaimed, her curiosity growing.

"Keep the voice down. That I can't tell you."

"Ohhh, come on."

"No, maybe someday, but not today." Gregory was adamant. "I don't know much, probably just enough to have me killed if I'm not careful."

Dani kept still. She didn't want to let her abductors know she was awake just yet—this information—priceless. The woman whose seat she had taken back at Starbucks was Jane Russell. She had been mistaken for this Jane Russell. What did all this mean? For one, this meant the attack was not meant for her, and Jack was safe. It also meant she would have to become Jane Russell. And the more she knew about Jane, the better.

Dani remembered seeing her bag fly under the van—with her ID. Her abductors did not have her ID, which was a very good thing.

The attendants at the front of the plane moved towards Gregory and Jody.

"I expect these women will wake up anytime now," one said.

"I've checked their vital signs prior to take-off. They're all stable," another responded.

"Dr. Pitt, what if they ask to use the facilities?" the attendant addressed as Jody asked. "These are women after all, and it has been more than five hours since anyone of them has relieved herself."

"Then let them relieve themselves. It's not like they'll be going anywhere. One at a time, of course." Dr. Pitt continued his rounds. "#6, our Jane Russell, she seems quite unusual.

Certainly not the typical woman requested. What's her story again? Refresh my memory." Dr. Pitt directed his question towards the male attendant, Gregory.

Gregory looked at his clipboard. His voice, monotone as if reading a grocery list. "She's suicidal, has made three attempts to end her life in the last two years, never been married, no kids, one estranged sister, prescription drug abuse, and this next one is interesting, has a lengthy record for shoplifting and pick pocketing—a little miss Klepto."

Gregory indicated to speak privately with Dr. Pitt. Together they talked in quiet tones.

Dani decided that this would be a good time to make herself known. She moved and groaned slightly.

"She's coming to," Jody whispered.

"Keep her calm, reassure her; everything's going to be OK. Got that, Jody?"

"Copy that."

Dani groaned. "Who are you? Where am I?"

"I'm here to ensure you have a safe flight."

"Safe flight...safe flight to where? I'm supposed to be..." Dani caught herself mid-sentence and coughed. She had almost said, 'supposed to be meeting Jack.'

Jody paused. "We're off to a resort of a sort."

"I'm supposed to be..." Dani hesitated. "...gettin' my hair done," Dani replied, her voice sluggish like one who's had a little too much to drink.

"Sure, sure, we'll see to it that you get your hair done. Just a little messed up, are we?" Jody said.

"I know I's messy. I tol you, I've a hair appoinmen." Dani intentionally exaggerated slurring sounds. "I never get to get my hair done, and today was my day. Do you know what it's like?"

Dani snuck a glance out the window and was surprised to see a white, snow-covered mountains as far as she could see. Judging from the setting sun, she deduced that they were flying North.

"Well, no I guess I don't know what it's like. But I can assure you we have some great things planned for you. Everything's going to be OK."

"Yeah, right. I don't understand. Why the handcuffs?" Without waiting for a reply, Dani continued, "I need to use the bathroom." She expressed urgency as she tried to stretch and free herself from the restraints.

"Of course. You realize you will have to cooperate—no funny business. I wouldn't want you to get hurt or anything." Jody whispered the last part of her sentence.

"Hurt?!" Dani gave the woman a shocked look, her eyes wide with fright and nodded compliantly. She wasn't surprised by the threat but knew she needed the woman to think she was. She also wasn't about to do anything stupid, especially with a full bladder.

Jody released Dani from her restraints and pointed her towards the rear of the plane. Then followed close behind as Dani swayed her way to the lavatory.

Sitting in the tiny cubical, Dani took in her cramped surroundings. She had no idea what she was looking for. Her head was pounding, and she shook all over. She was having trouble thinking clearly. *Stupid drugs. Not used to this stuff. Good thing I'm in shape.*

After relieving herself, Dani splashed cool water on her face, then looked at her reflection in the mirror. *I look awful.* She had seen better days, that was for certain.

Something hard tapped the side of the washbasin. *No! Yes! Can it be?...* Dani reached into her inside coat pocket. *Unbelievable! No one found my cell?! Or did they. If not, that means "whoever" didn't frisk me too well, or at all, and that means they're amateurs. Wait. No, these are not amateurs. Those two hoods who kidnapped me, they are amateur grunts, but not these guys. These are no amateurs. This—cell phone here—is more likely a God thing. Yes, it's got to be a God thing. God!* She hadn't thought about God for a long time. Another area of neglect—unlike Jack, who had this unwavering faith. Something he picked up after Bentley nearly died in his arms, something Dani didn't fully understand, but deep down, wished she could.

With trembling fingers, Dani tried to press the speed dial. Her fingers fumbled, and she nearly dropped the phone. Muttering to herself, she tried again. She waited. The chances of connecting were slim, but there was that chance. At that moment, she was never more grateful for her satellite phone, a gift from Jack. (Special compact edition through Jack's Navy Seal connections) Maybe just maybe...

SCENE 9

THE PHONE CALL

Jack, Chief Copper and Special Agents Staner, Miller and Conner are at the Well's residence. Tracing equipment and recorders are ready for the possibility kidnappers will make contact.

The phone rings.

Jack's jaw tightened, and his face turned hard, steely-cold. "Heads up. This could be them…"

"Jack Wells here," his voice authoritative, steady and strong.

"Jack." Dani's voice was barely above a whisper. "Jack, Jack, Listen..."

"Who is this?"

"It's me. Dani. I've got to keep my voice down, so listen up."

Jack put the phone on speaker mode. "Dani! It's Dani! Where are you, Dani?"

"Listen, just listen, I don't have much time. Here's what you need to know. The interior resembles a Challenger jet. We're flying North —maybe slightly North East. Nothing but mountains and snow— clear skies."

"Go on," Jack said. "You getting this, guys?" They nodded affirmatively.

"There are four plus two pilots, who I'll call captors; two men, two women, and there are six of us abducted women on board… We're the "packages." Jack, are you getting this?"

"Yes, yes … Packages? Six women?! That's strange. We've not come across reports of other missing persons."

"For good reason," Dani added. She groaned as a dizzy wave hit her. Taking a deep breath, she continued, "These women are all wasted. Nobody is going to be looking for them any time soon. They're either druggies, homeless or prostitutes or who knows what."

"So what are they doing with you? And what about you? Are you OK?"

"So far, just a little messed up from the drugs, that's all," Dani answered. "I'll be fine, just need some time. Check with Jason at Starbucks. Ask him about a woman sitting at a window table, facing south far right corner. I think their actual target was having a coffee just before I got there. I took her seat after she left. She was wearing a similar coat to mine and has the same color, length of hair as I do. I'm #6, Jane Russell, it seems."

"#6 Jane Russell. Give me more—everything you've got so far," Jack said.

"From their conversations, we've been picked for some kind of project."

"What's the project?" Jack queried.

"The 'Spy or Die Project.'" Some world intervention project of a sort. And don't ask me what that's all about because I don't have a clue."

The phone crackled. "We're breaking up, Jack. Looks like this is it. They've got guns, Jack."

"No, Dani, Dani! Names—give me names." The phone beeped. It's about to die. "What kind of guns?"

"Dr. Pitt, Gregory, Jody—that's it. Yes, serious ammo. These guys are serious; I'm canning the phone—can't risk them finding it."

"Code word...are you listening? Can you hear me?" Jack was urgent now, realizing he might never hear from or see his wife again.

"Code—'can the phone' is all I can think of right now. OK?"

The phone beeped again. " 'Can the phone' will work. I'll find you. I WILL find you," Jack yelled. "Remember, your skills. Keep your head on straight."

"I will, and I know you wi...."

The satellite phone died.

"She's canning the phone," Jack said, brushing his thick salt and pepper hair back from his forehead.

Silence reigned in the room—the agents standing by look questioningly at each other.

After what seemed like an eternity, Agent Miller said, "She was calling from the aircraft washroom."

Jack nodded.

"She actually had her phone on her!? How did that happen?" Agent Staner commented.

"Beats me. Got to be a God thing, is all I can say."

"Or it could be a setup—or these guys are total morons. But, something tells me they are not. And then again, it could be a God thing, as you say."

"Yes, she's dumping the phone down the toilet." Jack looked into the receiver. "Good move, Dani," he said. "She had no other choice."

Bentley whined.

"I know, boy—Dani's in big trouble. We'll find her, won't we partner?"

High in the sky in the tiny aircraft lavatory, Dani took a deep breath and dropped the phone into the toilet. She flushed. Strangely, at that moment, an unexpected peace came over Dani. Something shifted. The only way she could describe it was a strange feeling of calm and confidence came over her.

Dani took a few more deep breaths and stepped out of the washroom, slowly making her way to her seat. She still felt weak and dizzy. She would have to play along and be Jane Russell for now. *Who exactly is this Jane Russell?*

For now, whoever she is, Jane Russell is tired and not feeling very well. Jane Russell should probably rest like the other five women.

Dani noted how content they looked, in a deep drug-induced sleep, oblivious to their surroundings.

"You look a little tired, Ms. Russell," Jody commented as she snapped Dani's handcuffs back on and buckled her up. "A good sleep will help. You've got plenty of time for a nice nap before we get to our destination. Water will also help. Here, drink this."

Gratefully Dani drank the water and closed her eyes. She would sleep. She would need the rest if she were going to win at this game. Win she would, she determined, now that she had straightened a few things out with the God of the universe, whom Jack always told her, takes care of his own. Sleep came quickly for Dani.

Four hours later, they reached their destination.

SCENE 10

THE INVESTIGATION

Jack looks over the notes he scribbled down while talking to his wife. Then goes over them with the Chief.

"Whoever these guys are, they screwed up. They were supposed to pick up some woman named Jane Russell, not Dani. Agent Miller, can you play the recording for us, please, before I head out to the airport to check on flight plans. Chances are they didn't follow their flight, but we'll cover all the bases just in case."

"Copy that, Colonel Wells."

Listening to the recording, hearing Dani's voice was difficult. The realization her life was in serious jeopardy hit him hard. "We've got pretty much everything we need for now," Jack said.

"It's the airport then. We'll take my cruiser," the Chief said. Agent Conner, would you contact headquarters with the latest? Keep me posted. Special Agents Miller and Staner, you'll be looking for a Jane Russell. Find out who this woman is, and check the streets. Bring her in. There must be some word out there on these other five missing women.

"All either homeless, street workers, with no next of kin, or all of the above. Get a hold of that Jason fellow again—our Starbucks boy. We could use him on this one. This Jane Russell woman just might be a regular if we're lucky. That would explain the surveillance cameras shut down that night."

Agents Miller and Staner nodded, picked up their things and headed out the door. "Well, we know Dani's alive," Miller stated.

"Um, but for how long. Once they, whoever 'they' might be—once they learn Dani isn't their target, things aren't going to go too well for her," Staner replied.

"True, but she's a very capable woman," Miller countered. Got some serious training and all. Sounds like she's got her head together despite what she's been through."

"I hope you're right," Staner answered. "Just saying, I wouldn't want to be her right now. Even with all the things she's got going for her, chances aren't good."

"You don't know Jack Wells. He's got quite a reputation, Navy Seal and then some. Course it could all be hype. Something tells me not. Everyone needs a hero, and he's our hero. Who knows what he can do. They say he single-handedly captured a platoon—some say he's a regular terminator!!"

"Seems like much too nice a guy for that."

"Does, doesn't he. Guess we'll see, but from what I've heard, I want to be on his side. He headed up the Swat Team down in San Diego after serving in the military. They say he retired after police dog Bentley took a hit for him. Got religion too. Had enough, I guess. Into some youth training project now."

"Good for him. Sounds like he deserves retirement."

SCENE 11

A LEAD FROM UNION STREET

Jack and Bentley join Chief Copper in his police cruiser. Bentley is sitting in the back seat, his muzzle in the space between the two front seats. He whines softly. His ears perk forward as he listens to the police radio chatter, head tilted to the side, a thin stream of drool slides from the corners of his jowls.

"Looks like Bentley's not too impressed with retirement."

"I think he misses the action as much as I do. Retirement came too early for this K9 officer. It's all coming back, heh buddy?"

Bentley's responded with an enthusiastic bark that splattered spittle everywhere.

"OK, that's just gross..."

"You think!"

A radio transmission interrupted the light-hearted banter.

Police Dispatcher:
510, a Mrs. Heather Benson, 6345 Union Street, just called in to

report a white van with at least two male occupants, travelling at excessive speeds, yesterday at approximately 10:30 hours. The description of the stolen vehicle matches the one used in Dani Well's abduction. Repeat, 6345 Union Street."

"That's by the waterfront. There's a couple of abandoned warehouses down that area," Chief Copper said.

Dispatcher: "Mrs. Benson's boy and a couple of neighbour kids were playing soccer in the back alley when this incident occurred. The mother and her son, Jimmy, reported the van nearly ran the kids over. She sounded pretty upset."

The Chief turned on the flashers as he pressed his foot on the accelerator. "We are going to pay a visit to the Benson home."

SCENE 12

THE SOCCER TEAM & SOCCER MOM

Before turning onto Union Street, the Chief turns off his flashers and slows down to reach the speed limit.

"Here we are, 6345 Union Street. Not too shabby. Nice little home. It could use some repairs, though," the Chief said.

Jack looked out the open passenger window at the little bungalow; uncluttered yard, a decorative clay pot by the entry. "They're not renters. Too well-kept yard for renters," he observed. "This is one of the few residential areas in the city that is reasonably well-kept. And mainly homeowners, thanks to our mayor and all his efforts these past few years. He's made significant efforts to improve these parts. Good quality low-income housing, and we need those. As you well know, some of the young men in our program come from these parts."

"I sent several delinquents your way last year. I admire what you and your pastor friend are doing. You've got what it takes, that's for sure. Religion's never done much for me, but for some, it's a game-changer. I think I'll take the back alley where those kids were playing," the chief added as he eased the cruiser around the corner and into the alley.

"From here, you can see the waterfront and tops of the Lower Durmish River warehouses."

"Looks like our alley soccer team's got a game going on again today," Jack said. "One of those kids has got to be Jimmy."

Just then, Heather Benson stepped out the back door and yelled, "Jimmy, you've got ten minutes, then you do your chores. Got that?"

"Awe, Mom. We're winning. Fifteen minutes. Please, Mom?"

"Ten minutes." Heather noticed the cruiser, now in park.

The Chief and Jack exited the cruiser. Jack gave Bentley the stay order; the back window left fully opened. Bentley stuck his head out the window and kept his eyes on Jack. The men made their way towards Mrs. Benson.

One of the boys kicked the ball towards Jack. "We could use another player. You wanna join?"

Jack kicked the ball back with enthusiasm. "Love to, but we are here on a rather urgent mission."

"An urgent mission? Is someone in trouble? We all been really good, officer. Or, maybe you want our help?" the kid asked, his eyes wide with curiosity.

"A mission that has something to do with the van that nearly wiped out your soccer game yesterday. And yes, we think maybe you can be of help."

"That's cool. Officer Mr., that van racing through here like that was scary. My friend Brandon, he nearly got hit. It's like he felt it. It was so close."

By now, the kids had crowded around Jack, and as if on cue, each began relating, with great animation, his or her version of what happened.

"You all looking for me?" Mrs. Benson interrupted.

"Mrs. Benson?" Chief Copper asked. "Heather Benson? We'd like to speak briefly with you. I'm Chief Copper, and this is one of my men, Jack Wells. We're following up on a report you called in; about someone racing through here at excessive speed yesterday morning, driving a white van."

"Well, you took my call seriously. I thought you might not, cause nobody actually got injured. Yes, it is about that speeding van. These boys need somewhere to play their games, and this is what we got. You see that. No park anywhere near this place, and most of the time, there's no problem. Pretty much everyone in these parts pays attention and respects our boys` soccer field."

"Yes, Ma'am, and by the look of things, your boy's got some skills going for him. Jimmy, right?"

Jimmy smiled.

"Everyone, you can keep playing," Jimmy's mother instructed. "If we need you, we'll call, so stick around."

"OK, Mrs. Benson." The gang somewhat reluctantly went back to their game.

Heather returned her attention to the Chief. "Yes, that's my boy, Jimmy. And thanks for noticing. I think he's got some good skills too. Not to brag or anything, but truth is I've taught him pretty much everything he knows."

The chief smiled. "No doubt you have. So you played soccer?"

"College league. Intercollegiate Athletics for Women. Chapel Hill, North Carolina."

"That's impressive!" Jack moved to join in the conversation.

"What's impressive to one may not be to another, but thanks. Listen, why don't you come on in, and I'll answer your questions. I can make coffee. You interested?"

"Sounds great," the Chief answered as they followed Heather into the tiny kitchen. "We could use a little pick-me-up."

Rustic, utilitarian, very efficient kitchen, Jack observed. *A woman with some organizational skills.* Jack's observation skills training was ingrained; he continually evaluated his surroundings, taking in and processing information.

"Those kids out there," Heather said, "most of them don't have much going for them, so I teach them a few soccer skills now and then. Give them a safe place to play, and I get to keep an eye on my boy. Jimmy, he's only ten. Wish I could do better, but I do what I can do."

"Seems to me you're doing a whole lot of good," Jack responded. "From what I see, Jimmy's blessed to have a mother like you. Might I ask, does he have a dad?"

Heather held the coffee pot over the Chief's cup. A trace of sadness momentarily swept over her face. "His father died in a work accident two years ago. Insurance won't pay out—but that's a story for another time." Heather poured the coffee into the Chief's mug, then proceeded to fill Jack's.

"I'm very sorry for your loss," Jack responded. "That is a significant loss for both you and your son.

The Chief nodded in agreement.

"He was a good man," Heather continued. "He worked hard, and he loved his family, and that's the good memories we've got to take with us, wherever life takes us. I'm thankful for that. But you didn't come here to listen to my life story. What I do want you to know is my neighbors and me, we want to keep this place safe for our children. So, when someone comes barreling down our back alley with no regard for our children and could have killed any one of them or more, I got to do something, so I called you."

"We're glad you did, Mrs. Benson. "I'm just wondering why it took you till today to make the report."

"Yeah, that. I was going to call yesterday but then thought no one's going to care anyway, so what's the use. I talked with some of my neighbors whose kids were involved, and they were right mad too. So when I couldn't sleep most of the night, I figured best to call. Least I did my part."

"Well, we are glad you did make that call. We're in the middle of an investigation, the details of which I am not at liberty to discuss, but I do want you to know this is very serious, and any information you might have will help."

"That serious, heh. I knew something wasn't right. Can't you tell me anything? Do I have to worry about the kids? Are we safe?"

"I can't divulge details at this time. The press will get ahold of this story soon enough, so keep an eye on the news. I'm sure you understand. You are safe. I'll have several of my officers assigned to patrolling this area until we get these guys."

"OK, I'll let the parents know, so they won't be worrying. Well, let's see, I was here at my kitchen window—right here by the sink," Heather began.

"I was washing up the breakfast dishes. I get this great view of the soccer field—I call the alley a soccer field because I've learned you get much further if you think big. And those kids, if they want to succeed, they gotta think like it's a soccer field.

"Dream about it. Do it right—you know— sorry, back to my report. So, I was here standing washing the breakfast dishes when I see the kids scramble for the sidelines an' jumpin' the fences and then this van comes barreling through, I say fifty clicks at least. No braking, nothing. If anything, the driver accelerated."

"And I see little Brandon—and it looks like he's not going to make it—I was sure he was going to get run over—and I screamed. It was a close call. It couldn't have been closer. I thought he'd been hit. And then I see Brandon hanging onto the fence, and he's not down on the ground, and I gasp with relief." Heather took a deep breath, her hand on her chest.

"So, I raced to the door," she continued, "and I ran like a crazy lady after that piece of trash, just thinking I might get the license plate number. He was way too far down the road for that, but I did get an M and L—I think that's what it was.

"I saw a driver and passenger, so I know there were at least two people in that van. The back windows were tinted, so I don't know if anyone else was inside. Jimmy and the others say they saw two males. You can ask them."

"Did you see any signage on the side of the van?"

"No. It was just plain and dirty with rusted parts."

"Is there anything else you can think of?"

"Oh, yes. The driver's window smashed in; still had glass pieces sticking out. That's pretty much it."

"Mrs. Benson, you have been a big help," the Chief said. "Thank you. If you think of anything else, please call me personally."

The Chief handed her his card.

Jack and the Chief moved to leave.

"Wait, Chief," Heather said. "I have a thought. Maybe, when you've got this thing solved and all, maybe you or one of your officers could drive by once in a while, check on the kids. Maybe even kick the ball around. They'd love it, and it'd do them a lot of good. Know I might be asking a lot, but it doesn't hurt to ask. They could use a good man around, even if it's once in a while. They'll be teenagers before we know it, if you know what I mean."

"I sure do, Mrs. Benson. It will be our pleasure. Let me work on that. I think I have just the man for the job. I'll get back to you on that by the end of next week. And, Mrs. Benson, if you ever need anything, if you ever have any trouble, give me a call."

SCENE 13

BENTLEY'S DISCOVERY

A force of officers swarm Seattle's Lower Durmish River area checking empty and abandoned warehouses for the white van. Two hours into the search, they are successful.

Bentley barks and scratches at one of the warehouse doors and that is how they locate the suspect's vehicle.

Bentley whined with excitement, sniffing and circling the abandoned beat-up, white van parked in a dilapidated but otherwise empty warehouse. Soon the place would be swarming with police detectives and forensics.

"Bentley's back on the job, I see," an agent commented.

"And he couldn't be more pleased," Jack responded. "Dani's scent is driving him crazy—she was here, and the trail ends here. Most likely transferred to another vehicle. Good to have you working with us, by the way, agent."

"Thank you, Sir. I'm honored to be part of this investigation. It looks like whoever it was, wiped the place clean. But you never know. One careless mistake is all we need."

A cell phone sang a catchy tune, and the agent pulled it from his pocket. "Better take this," he said.

A few seconds later, "Chief, they just found what they believe to be our two suspects, floating in the canal. Thing is, there was a third, a male in his twenties, wearing a jogging outfit. Not sure how he fits."

"Great! Not good. Not good at all. Now we know just how serious these people are and what they are capable of."

SCENE 14

PROJECT HEADQUARTERS

On the second floor of a non-descript, dated, two-story brick building near Seattle's Pike Place Market is the "non-existent" headquarters for Project Spy or Die. Across the street is a well-manicured and significant city park.

Two people stand in the shade under a tree in the park.

"OSD is up and running. As of today, following your orders, sir, all traces are covered, and the project is now in full swing."

"Good. Keep me posted on any significant changes. Other than that, you'll be contacted within the week regarding our next meet."

"Yes, sir."

Voices fade as they separate. One enters the building. The sign on the building—TurnKey Intelligence Operation. The other continues his walk in the park.

SCENE 15

INTRODUCTION TO THE
SPY OR DIE PROJECT

Seventy-two hours later.

The six abducted women are sitting in a sterile room. Two security guards stand behind them, along with two formidable guard dogs. One guard is positioned at the exit.

The women have been cleaned up, although most appear to be in different stages of withdrawal, except for Dani. Her captors address her as #6 Jane Russel.

"My name is Dr. Frankel. I understand you've been through a difficult few days. Considering how you spend MOST of your days—these past few days here should rank pretty favorable, wouldn't you agree? You are resilient and resourceful, and I might add highly intelligent women. You are also survivors. The good news for you today is, your lives are about to change dramatically—and for the better."

Dr. Frankel paused and adjusted his black-rimmed glasses, then pulled a pen from the pocket of his white lab coat. He looks to be in his thirties. Although he has the appearance of an absent-minded professor, he could be described as quite handsome.

Reminds me of Harrison Ford—the professor in the movie, **Raiders of the Lost Ark**, Dani observed.

She wondered where this Dr. fit in this bizarre Spy or Die Operation. By now, Dani understood this "business" is a secretive and extremely dangerous, deadly one. She observed that underneath the lab coat, the Dr. appeared to be in pretty solid shape. No belly, strong upper body, straight military walk.

That was it. *The walk, the talk, they all tell a great deal about someone. He could be much more threatening than he appears. He comes across as genuinely kind, concerned, understanding. It could all be a front to get us to relax. After all, we are a project. Then again, maybe he is a recruit as well. Just another pawn in this sinister, mysterious game. Maybe he doesn't want to be here either.*

"Today I will introduce you to the program. By the time we're finished, you will understand why you are here, and you will be clear about the expectations we have. You will be delighted to be here." The Dr. paused.

He looked into the staring-in-disbelief eyes of the six women facing him. *These women have no idea what they've got coming. They will thank me one day, one day soon. As long as I...* The Dr. clicked his pen several times on the electronic gadget in his hand. *There is no reason whatsoever this project will not be a 100% success.*

Dani observed the strange gadget in the Dr.'s hand, noting it responded to touch and revealed electronic images and text in an instant.

That's an incredible little gadget the Dr.'s got there. I wonder if Jack's seen one of those. It has a keyboard hidden somewhere, and with a tap of his pen, he calls up images. These guys are way ahead of the game.

The Dr.'s incredible little gadget, which would become known as an iPad, would make its entry into the general public some eight years later when it would be sold on the market for $500.

The doctor proceeded. "You have been selected for a project with far greater importance and significance than you can envision. Why me, you ask. I'm glad you asked that question.

"Firstly because you, each one of you, as I said earlier, is resilient, creative, resourceful and highly intelligent. All of you have forgotten who you are, and some of you have never even had the opportunity to know who you really are or who you could become. In the next few months, you will discover things about yourself, good and exciting things about yourself you never dreamed possible."

"Seems to me you've been dreaming just a little too much," the woman identified as #2, Marcie, commented.

"Yeah," added Gracie, the woman identified as #4, "What've you been smoking? Give me some of that Burrito (a street name for weed)."

This brought snickers from the women.

The Dr. ignored them, although he offered a slight smile before continuing. "Interestingly enough, Gracie, you will never want to smoke Burritos, or take drugs of any sort, again."

"Right!" Gracie said. "You ain't never been there, man. What you talkin' 'bout?"

The women begin muttering amongst themselves—except Dani, who continued to observe intently.

"Man, how am I going to survive another day listening to this crap?" Kelly #1 said.

"Shut up," Becky #3 said. "I wanna hear what this dude has to say. I got nothin' better to do today 'cept curl up in that sweet bed and sleep."

"How are you going to shut it off, Doc.?" Gracie asked. "You expect me to believe I don't want that stuff? That's my life. I can't exist without it, and I know that for a fact. I've been without for way too long now, and so let's get to the point; what's it going to take to get some?"

"Yeah, where'd you get your degree? Dr. Frankel. Dr. of what?" Marcie asked.

"Sounds more like Dr. Frankenstein. You don't know what it's like to be an addict. You've never been in my hell pit!"

Dr. Frankel raised his hand, and surprisingly, the women went quiet. "I do understand your disbelief. Short of a miracle, you would not survive. You're right. Most of you, except for one, (he looked at Dani—she held his gaze without a flinch) would die. Tell me, why are you not dead then?"

No one responded.

"As you know, during the past few days, you've been tested, probed, analyzed and studied. We know everything there is to know about your body. Every injury you ever sustained, every flaw in your cell formation, every minute detail there is to know about your composition and chemistry make-up, right down to your DNA. We have everything documented.

"For what purpose? Each one of you is an individual 'project' within a much larger project. And as part of this project, we are about to discover that no matter how old you are, what condition you are in, unless you're dead, we can re-build you into the perfect person you were or could have been at age 25. With some seriously impressive, additional qualities, which we will discuss at a later date.

"That, ladies, is our goal, and with or without your cooperation, is what will happen."

The women stared in disbelief at Dr. Franklin. The possibility of becoming youthful, energetic, maybe even beautiful again, was far beyond comprehension at this stage in their lives.

This Dr. Frankel is an even bigger nutcase than any of the women in this room. Dani stifled a snicker. *This would be humorous if it weren't so crazy.*

"Heh, this is getting just too weird." Sandra, "project" #5, broke the silence. She sighed and snorted as she sunk her boney frame into her seat, shook her head and gave the Dr. a look that said: *"You are one crazy dude."*

"So, when you've reached this goal, and your project is complete, we get to go back to where ever it is we wanna be, right?" Dani queried.

"Not exactly," the Dr. answered.

"Not exactly means no to me," Dani returned. "What we have here is kidnapping, abuse of power, deception, fraud, exploitation. I haven't agreed to this."

"Oh, Ms. Russell. In time you will thank me:"

"So there is more to this 'project' than just making me into some adrenaline-addicted, beautiful and bewitching superhuman genius? You said you'd tell us everything. What's the rest then?"

Dr. Frankel chuckled. "I'm going to love this," he said. "We also know your history. There isn't anything we don't know about you. None of you have anything of substance or meaning to go back to. That is precisely why each of YOU was selected.

"For instance, Jane here tried to commit suicide again recently— for the third time You have no family, except for one estranged sister, no brothers, parents are dead, hooked on prescription drugs, you like to take things that don't belong to you, and your life sucks. Need I continue? Your lucky break is to have been selected.

"Gracie. Let's talk about you for a minute. I don't think you want to go back to the ghetto, the fights and the beatings, not to mention the constant search for your next fix. You—he pointed his pen at Gracie, have had fifty-seven broken bones in total. Nasty."

Gracie cringed and slunk into her chair. "I lost count," she muttered. "The bastard."

"Becky. Sandra, Marcie—you'll never have to work the streets again. Now, isn't that good news? And to take care of your drug dependency?

"Kelly, you know it's only a matter of time before your ex finds you. He nearly succeeded in terminating you; you took a gunshot wound to the chest, lost your left breast. He left you for dead. Remember? You miraculously survived and have been hiding ever since."

Kelly instinctively placed a hand onto her left breast.

The room went deathly silent. Somewhere a pin dropped, and everyone heard it.

"We also know that each one of you scored well above 135 on your high school IQ test."

"So, we're a super-smart, 'highly-gifted' sorry bunch. What's the deal then? Why us?" Becky spoke up.

"Ladies...here's the clincher. In exchange for all your years of pain and suffering, I will transform you into trained operators, yes gorgeous and super-smart spies for one powerful American billionaire technologist, whom you don't want to disappoint.

"What the—spies! You've got to be joking—right?" Becky responded. "I'm a losin' hooker, and you're gonna make me into a spy! Go babe!! This ought to be good!"

"That's just nonsense. And what's this American stuff anyway?" Kelly asked. "I'm no American citizen. Not my favorite…"

"You have something against Americans?" Sandra responded. "My great, great grandfather was a Civil War hero. I wouldn't be…."

"Oh, get a grip. I'm try'n to put two and two together, and you're bringing up some stupid dead man. You're not even half as smart as you look, you idiot."

In a moment, Sandra lost all composure and, in one smooth movement, jumped out of her seat and tackled Kelly. The two smashed into Becky and Marcie, and soon there was a regular free-for-all, drag-down cat-fight. At first, Dani avoided the brawl, but after second thoughts, she decided to jump in. *What the hey— if I'm going to be Jane Russell, I better play the part.*

Multiple bruises and bloody noses later.

SCENE 16

LEVERAGE

Eight weeks later.

"Well, Ms. Russell. Jane Russell. You are in remarkable shape for forty-seven years of age, quite unlike your comrades. They're responding as expected. You—you are well beyond what's expected. Curious, isn't it. You will turn out to be quite a specimen. Perhaps my crowning achievement!" Dr. Frankel spoke frankly to Jane. "The next stages of your transformation may produce some minor discomforts, but twenty-four hours in this super "Hyperbaric Chamber" will minimize the pain. Your recovery time will be oh... 5-10% of the normal recovery time I designed this fabulous, one-of-a-kind, never-been-done-before machine myself, I might add."

"Quite remarkable, Dr. You are a very clever man. Tell me more about your inventions." Dani stood in front of the mirror and analyzed her body. As promised, the treatments she had been subjected to for the past two weeks were beginning to metamorphose her body into a youthful, even shapely figure. Birthmarks, moles, skin tags, even wrinkles and brown spots all disappeared. She listened to the doctor brag as she checked her hands, her skin, her feet.

"You are transforming into an extraordinarily, remarkably beautiful woman.

"Thing is, you were quite extraordinary before all this—but the youthfulness, the reversing of time. In the next eight weeks, you'll have a completely new anatomy."

Dr. Frankel reached out his hand to touch Dani's cheek.

Instinctively she shrank back. Her heart began to race. *Not the scar! The scar stays. He will not take that from me. Not my reminder of Papa, who loved me. Of the day he caught me in his arms when I jumped from the second-story window of our house filled with smoke and flames.. It was so far down and I was so scared.* Eight-year-old Dani, at the instructions of her frantic father yelling at her from below her window, had shattered her bedroom window with a chair. Shreds of glass that still lodged in the window frame were the cause of several deep lacerations on her arms and legs as well as the one on her cheek. But her Papa had saved her.

"The scar worries you, does it? There are memories there. Soon it will be gone. Soon the memories will all be gone and replaced with new ones."

Dani composed herself, relaxed and smiled. "I see," she replied. But her heart sank knowing this was one battle she would probably lose.

"Here, take a look at these images."

Frankel showed her some artistic images on a computer monitor.

"Umm...this is quite something," Dani responded. "It's like I'm 25 again...but in a different kind of way, a super-human kind of way. You were going to tell me about your inventions. I'm interested, you know."

"Perhaps too interested."

Dani ignored the comment, although her guard went up instantly.

Dr. Frankel persisted. He pushed his chair back from his desk. "Your DNA. It doesn't match the DNA sample I received before your arrival. Your photo, there are striking similarities. But Jane Russel does not have the scar."

Dani hesitated ever so slightly. *Here we go...*

"So? A picture can be altered and maybe even incorrectly submitted. As for DNA, it probably got switched or something like that. It happens all the time in the medical field. Someone probably messed up big time," she responded.

"Someone messed up, alright. Thing is, I know you're not Jane Russell." The Dr. paused to let the revelation sink in. He waited for a response, and when none came, he asked, "Who are you?"

"Dr. Frankel, you know who I am. What do you mean?"

"Don't mess with me, Ms. Russell," retorted Dr. Frankel. "Picture and DNA aside, how about answering a few questions. Where were you born? What school did you attend? What's your mother's maiden name?"

"Why do I need to give you that information? You know all that stuff."

"Stop with the lies. You may not realize it, but you are alive today because I am the only one who knows about this. In fact, I lied for you. Mess-ups are not allowed in this business."

"Aren't we under surveillance? What game are you playing?" Dani's voice was lowered to a whisper.

"No cameras or mics in my domain. I don't allow it. We can speak freely here."

No cameras! And he just admitted he lied about me. That's leverage—time to play one of my cards. "OK, so I'm not Jane Russell. My guess is, you're the only one going to know," Dani continued. You've let it go this long. Look, I'm in the program; with the program. What does it matter? I'm Jane Russell. I'm beginning to like her. Look at what you've done with her. Anyway, you should know, I can be of significant benefit to you. I do have a few things to offer."

"Really. You have things to offer? Such as?"

"You keep Jane Russell safe, and I'll let you know. For now, I think we best keep her our secret."

"You're going to have to do better than that. Be straight with me. Things can get ugly if you don't."

The Dr.'s communication device beeped. "Looks like I've got to attend to something, but don't think this conversation is over. We will be talking. The Dr. ran his hands down Jane's arms. His face softened and glowed with pride. "You are so different from the others. There is something uniquely intriguing about you. You've responded much quicker than expected, and yes, you are quite a prize. I hope to use you as my prototype." The Dr. stepped back, his face back to being stern and reserved. "And that is why, for now, our secret is safe with me."

Dani breathed a sigh of relief. "Thank you, Dr." *I need to sound convincing, be convincing.* "You are amazing. So incredibly talented. You are a true genius. I have never met anyone quite like you."

Dr. Frankel took both Dani's hands into his and pressed them to his lips. "That's what I admire about you. You know genius when you see it. I'll be back shortly. I have something to attend to—why don't you relax. Come, make yourself comfortable in my recliner. "We have lots to talk about. Rubin here," the Dr. nodded towards the Rottweiler guarding the door, "he'll keep you company until I return."

Dani smiled and made her way to the rich chestnut-colored, Italian leather recliner. *Probably this is where he gets his inspiration. Nice. I wouldn't mind one of these in my living room—if I ever get back there. No, when I get back there.* Dani slid into the seat, closed her eyes and sighed. "Very comfortable. Yes, I could use one of these."

"I'm glad you approve," the Dr. replied as he closed the door behind him.

Dr. Frankel left the room and Dani's smile faded. *Think, think... I'm playing him to survive right now. God, help me. I'm buying me some time, but this has got to stop.* Dani went to the sink, washed her hands and splashed cold water on her face. *I've got to keep the Dr. on my side, and I've also got to get him to stop this nonsense with his romantic fantasies. I guess I'm just going to have to tell him, aren't I? So, what are you going to do?*

And that's when Dani's plan took on a new dimension. Her attention turned to Rubin. She sensed a prompting. *Ah, yes, time to make my dog whisperer move.* Dani had always been in tune with animals. She spent ten of her younger years working with and learning from one of the best guard dog trainers in the country. She knew dogs, and she knew breeds. She was confident she could master any one of these guard dogs, regardless of their training. *Time to play that card.*

With a firm voice, Dani commanded Rubin to "Komm." Rubin looked momentarily confused, his expression almost comical. At the repeated command, he lowered his head and moved obediently to her side. Dani praised him. But as she made a move to leave the room, the dog reacted and moved to interfere. "Rubin. Nein. Platz." Slowly Rubin lowered his belly to the floor. "Bleibe."

This time Rubin stayed put.

Dani opened the door, stepped out and closed it behind her. She waited for two minutes, then went back into the room to find Rubin where she had left him in the obedient, down-stay position. She praised him, and the dog shoved his nose into the palm of her hand.

Satisfied she had established her authority with Rubin, Dani had the dog return to his position guarding the door. She returned to the recliner, where she waited for Dr. Frankel to return.

By the time the Dr. returned, it was time for Improvised Weapons training session, and their "further discussion" would have to wait.

Dani was relieved.

SCENE 17

THE BILLIONAIRE TECHNOLOGIST

Dr. Frankel and two assistants are conversing with a fourth party via an internet screen in a sound-proof, vault-like office. The fourth man behind the screen is the one Dr. Frankel is accountable to and who is ultimately in charge of Project Spy or Die.

Mr. Bacardi, a billionaire technologist, known to be eccentric, is suspected by extremists and conspiracy theory activists to be behind various underhanded and evil plots against humanity, all in the name of power and control.

"Mr. Bacardi, sir. Things are running 100% as planned." Dr. Frankel spoke. "The Assets will be ready for assignment as scheduled. Everything is running as planned."

Bacardi nodded. "I should expect so. I don't need to remind you this project leaves zero room for error. One mistake, and the project will be terminated. You know what that means, Dr. Frankel, don't you?" Bacardi's pointed his pen towards the men at the screen with emphasis.

An electrical charge ran through Dr. Frankel. Although Bacardi was communicating via computer screen, he might as well be in the room.

"Yes, Sir, I am aware." Beads of sweat begin to pool on the Dr.'s forehead. "Yes, Sir, I do, Sir! There will be no errors, Sir. I give you my word."

"Right then. Keep up the good work, men."

The screen went blank.

Dr. Frankel drew in a deep breath, then let it out slowly. He wiped his forehead with his sleeve.

SCENE 18

FACE OFF FACE ON

Today Dani and her five companions choose their facial features. Each of them is limited to five options from which to choose. Dani is not at all happy about changing her facial features, especially knowing she will lose the scar.

Considering her situation, she knew it was silly to grieve over something as trivial as a scar, something most women have cosmetic surgery to remove. But she wasn't "most women." She never was or would be.

Dani took her time, trying to decide which of the five options most suited her, was the closest to her own, and, more importantly, one Jack would be comfortable with. As far as she was concerned, she was NOT destined for a life of espionage. She will go back home, one way or another.

For the other women, this is exciting, mixed with a smidgen of misgivings. But as for Dani, who was never discontent with her looks, she has significant misgivings.

On the lighter side, they can choose their hair color and style, which must be different from their norm.

Dani decides on the hairstyle she intended to get the day she was abducted. She has every intention of being reunited with her husband and knows he will have discovered the clipping when going through her bag. With all the changes, she wants to make sure he knows without a doubt; she is his Dani. She chooses sharp facial features; a defined jawline, high cheekbones, prominent brow bone, full lips but not obvious or distracting, and intense piercing eyes.

The transformations continue.

The time had come—the time for the bandages to come off! The Jane Russell who stepped out of the Hyperbaric Chamber was, needless to say, mesmerizing. This new face would take some getting used to. She reminded herself she had the memory of her used-to-be self. She would adapt. She would embrace the changes. If she was going to survive, she would have to.

Dani looked at her fellow project comrades and could not resist a smile. What a team they were. But the smile quickly left. She knew she had a big job ahead of her if she was going to convince even one of these women to abandon the project and attempt to escape with her. From their perspective, that would be suicide. They also have nothing to lose by sticking with the program. From her perspective, she had everything to lose. Right now, they were feeling invincible.

Dani noticed each of the women had a small tattoo on their upper left shoulder. She observed each one was similar yet slightly different. *Some sort of identification my guess. I wonder what other identifying markers they left with us—in us. Yep, I've got one too.*

The Dr. interrupted her thoughts. "Operatives, introduce yourselves." At this point, the Dr. was the only one who knew who was who.

After the identity reveal, Dani noticed Gracie eyeing her. *Gracie's new features suit her to a T. Now, if we could only get along.*

She does not like me in the least. Dani could feel Gracie's hostility and competitiveness. *I wonder why she feels threatened by me. Maybe she knows something. But how? She can't possibly know that I'm not Jane—can she? Regardless, I'll need to stay on the alert.*

6:30 AM the next morning, Dani threw off the covers, slid out of bed and made her way to her bathroom. She yawned. Before looking in the mirror, she placed her hands on the sides of the sink and took a deep breath. "Today is the first day of the rest of my life, and I better get used to it."

She looked up at her new self-reflection in the mirror.

Her knees buckled! What she saw looking back at her shook her to the core. "Unbelievable!. This is awesome!" Overnight, the scar on Dani's cheek had mysteriously reappeared. "OK—this has got to be a sign. I AM going to get out of here. Even though Jack may not need this scar to know it's me, I do. I need it. I'm still Dani, and no matter what you do to me, you—you Dr. Frankel and all the rest of you power-hungry monsters, I will always be Dani." At that moment, Dani knew that she knew that she knew, no matter how many times the Dr. did a redo, and she knew he would, this scar wasn't going anywhere.

When Dr. Frankel saw the scar later that day, he was beside himself. "How is this possible? This has NEVER happened before!" the perplexed Dr. exclaimed. "I do not understand. What an unusual phenomenon. There is no possible logical reason why this scar is still on your face. We will do a redo. This is not acceptable."

Dani simply smiled and said, "Do as many redos as you like. This scar is not going anywhere. You are not going to win this one, Dr. Frankelstein."

"Well, we'll see about that."

SCENE 19

NOTHING BUT DEAD ENDS

Back at the station, with Bentley at his side, Jack and the Chief are in conversation.

"We've run out of options, Jack. Besides the real Jane Russell, we've not found a single trace of any of the other five abducted women. They didn't leave us any valuable clues. We've scoped the entire northern areas of the country. The Yukon, North West Territories, Alaska. Again, not a clue has turned up."

Visible behind them is an 8x10 of Dani, her name, aka Jane Russel, and the Project SOD written underneath. Jack ran his hand slowly over the photo. "It's been two months now, and we're no further ahead than when we started; at least that's how it appears. That doesn't make sense. We must be missing something."

"I thought we might make some headway when we found Jane Russell, but she was no help whatsoever. She had no idea what was meant for her. All we do know is that she profiles the category of women Dani said these people were after."

"At least she's getting some help now. With her new identity, and the friendships she's found in our little community, this beautiful woman is gaining confidence and strength day by day. And she's even been coming to Sunday morning service at our chapel."

"That's good news. Something good coming out of all this at least." The Chief paused before changing the topic, "Jack, I'm going to have to take my men off the priority list on this case, you realize that."

"I know," Jack answered. "I will keep on it though. I'm sure you understand."

"I wouldn't expect you to do anything else. If you get anything, anything at all, talk to me. I'm not closing the case, Jack, just taking it off the priority list. You do know I'm still with you on this one."

Jack nodded." You've done everything you could."

"In fact, Jack—I've been thinking, off the record, I'm going to make contact with Clay, Mac, Billy, Pete, Cam and JD. If anything comes up, we'll be ready. I couldn't think of better-qualified men to do the job."

"I owe you, Chief."

"It`s Lance—and you don't owe me a thing. We're way past that. We stick together—always."

"Semper Fi."

SCENE 20

HOPE COMES FROM THE MOST UNLIKELY

Jack is sitting in the Starbucks coffee shop in the spot where Dani sat the day she went missing. He muses over his Grande, then looks out the window across the street in the direction where the van was parked that fateful day.

Jason sauntered over to Jack. He placed two glasses of water on the table. "I'm real sorry, man," he said awkwardly.

"It wasn't your fault," Jack responded.

Jason cleared his throat. "Well, now that you're not interrogating, or maybe it was interviewing me, ahh—whatever it was, it doesn't matter. I know that was just part of the process. What I want to say is, I thought I'd; maybe you'd be OK if I talked to you on a more say, personal basis?"

"What's on your mind, son?" Jack raised the paper cup to his lips and took a sip.

"Your wife, Dani. She's one great lady—but then, that's nothing new to you—I just wanted you to know."

"Thanks."

"So you're the man she's so in love with."

"Ahum."

"Sorry, that was dumb, insensitive—whatever." Jason stumbled over his words. "I meant it must be nice to have someone who loves you as much as she loves you."

"I do agree. I am one lucky man. You are absolutely right. Have a seat."

Jason slid into the seat. "Look, I've wanted to talk to you. You're a religious guy, aren't you?"

"Not really."

"But, but you and this preacher man; you've got this youth project happening that's got everybody's attention, and well, I just assumed..."

"If by religious you mean I believe in God Almighty and I've got a personal relationship with His Son Jesus Christ, then yes, I've got some religion. You said you had something to say," Jack redirected.

Jason shifted uneasily. "I get it. I think. About this religious stuff and all. Anyway, sounds good to me. Yes, about what I wanted to say. I'm thinking you're giving up, and umm, I don't think you should be giving up. I presume you've tried praying and all? That was a stupid question. Of course, you have."

Jack smiled, a sad smile nevertheless. "I'm not giving up. And I've done my share of praying, believe me. Right now, I'm just listening. To be honest, I don't know where to go from here. I've run out of ideas. I have to admit I feel helpless. I've always known what to do... and now, here I am, without a clue."

Why am I telling this guy, some twenty years my junior, how I'm feeling? Because he deserves your honesty. Now, that's a thought. Unlike most people, he's got the intestinal fortitude to speak his mind to my face, something worth noting. Yes, that is worth noting. More to this guy than one might think.

"Well, I think that's probably a pretty common feeling in your situation." Jason's voice interrupted Jack's thoughts.

"Maybe I've been doing too much doing and not enough listening," Jack responded. "So I thought I'd do a little listening, and somehow I ended up here."

"That's a good thing," Jason responded. "I just wanted you to know. I've been lighting a candle for Dani every week."

"Thank you, Jason. I appreciate that."

Valentina, who was whipping up a couple of cappuccinos, watched the two men intently. Her hands shook ever so slightly, and her cheeks were unusually flushed. She served the two patrons their cappuccinos, made her way to Jack and Jason's table and blurted, "I have something to say."

Jack motioned for Valentina to sit down beside Jason across from him. "You too? Please, what is it you've got to say?"

"If I tell you, will you promise to help me?" Valentina appealed to Jack.

"I will if I can. It must be important. You are shaking like a leaf."

Valentina lowered her voice to a whisper. "That's because I have a secret." She paused and bravely continued, "I have to get this off my chest and do what's right."

"Go on," Jason urged. He was looking at her as if he had never really seen her until that very moment. She was much more interesting than he had been giving her credit for.

"I"...she hesitated as if not sure where to begin. "I've been having this dream. I have had it several times now, the same dream. It's about your wife. I don't know why YOU couldn't just have the dream and be done with it, but dreams are in my family and many times they come true."

She paused and went on. "Today I said, 'If I am supposed to tell Mr. Wells this dream, then I will have to have a sign. The sign I said would be that you, Mr. Jack Wells, would come into this coffee shop today, and you would have to sit right there, where your wife sat, that... that awful day.' And here you sit. And so I have no other options but to tell you. I believe what I have to say will bring you to her."

Jack was now leaning forward, curiosity written all over his face. "I'm listening."

"Do you believe in dreams, Mr. Wells?" she asked, prolonging what she was about to tell him.

"I do today—please, the dream."

"Your wife—she is in this place. I see her in this room, and it is like a hospital of some kind. People with white coats are walking around, and they are always doing the same thing. These people and machines are working on her, and she is changing until she looks like someone else, but it is her. I know it is still her. Then the dream changes and I see snow and ice and the letters A K L A V I K N E, scrolling across the scene. She stopped, then added, "And there is this one face that keeps showing up. An evil face, and his eyes are like a snake. There is great danger there."

Valentina took a deep breath. She tried to swallow, but her mouth was suddenly dry.

"Is there more?" Jason asked.

She nodded. They waited. Jason slid a glass of water to her.

"The next part has to do with the secret part. I'm in this dream, you see." Valentina looked at Jack without flinching. "Now, in the dream, we are all there, you, Jason, myself—by this place, this strange place, with security guards and dogs; big vicious dogs, and alarms and cameras everywhere. And I am scaling the wall. I scale this wall of ice to the top of what must be the roof of a five or six-story building covered in ice and snow. Everything is white, and there are no windows, just a mountain of pure ice—and that's where the dream ends."

"Well, up until the last part, it was pretty credible," Jason offered.

"You know nothing about me, Jason Whiting," Valentina remarked in a way that clearly implied she wished he was more interested in knowing her.

"That's quite the dream," Jack responded. "Those letters, A K L A V I K N E —they spell the name of an Inuit village about as far north as one can imagine. Aklavik. The N E— short for location North East—North East of Aklavik. Interesting. Dani said they were flying over snow-covered mountains. We've had military flying over much of the northern territories, but there are thousands of frozen wilderness miles to cover. A daunting task without some indication of where to focus the search."

"Now we have a clue!" Jason exclaimed excitedly. "We've got something to go on. Course this isn't enough for the police. They need facts, not dreams, but I think we're on to something."

"I think you're right, Jason. This is no chance meeting. Tell me, Valentina, explain your climbing this wall of ice?" Jack gently prompted.

"Here is where I need your help. You see—I am—(she paused a long pause) I am a professional cat burglar." She waited for her words to sink in.

"I see." Jack said after a long pause, then added, "I did NOT see that coming. But, you climbing the wall makes sense now. Go on."

"I come from a very prestigious family of cat burglars. I started very young. I came to this country to start a new life and get away from my past. I came under a different name and not legally—really. I have managed quite well for the past three years. Maybe this is the way to redeem myself. Maybe that's why I was chosen to have this dream."

"Is there more?"

"I think perhaps you are going to need me to help Dani and those other women escape. I am very good at what I do, by the way."

Jack looked at her intently while processing the anomalous information. "If you're right, and you have the skill sets you say you do—and I'm inclined to think you do, I will do whatever I can to help you stay in this country—legally. You have my word."

A look of relief spread over Valentina's face. "I know I'm right, and I can. As I said, I know a thing or two about dreams."

Now Jason was looking at Valentina with a great deal of admiration, an enchanted look in his eyes. This time, the two exchanged electrifying glances. *How could I have not noticed this exciting, beautiful creature before?*

"OK," Jack said slowly, thoughtfully. "I think I've got my answer. You two are part of this somehow. By the way Jason—Jason. Give it a rest 'til later."

Jason chuckled before reluctantly taking his eyes off Valentina.

He looked across the table at Jack, but his mind was on the captivating woman beside him. *Wow! What will my future look like?*

"I don't quite get it. What do **you** have to bring to the table, Jason? Why are you in her dream?"

Jason shrugged confidently. "I think I might just have something you need. Both of you come with me."

SCENE 21

TRANSFORMED AND TROUBLE'S A-COMIN'

Jane Russell's ultimate make-over is now complete. Her body is exquisitely sculpted, muscular yet feminine.

Next on the agenda, intense physical training. The Dr. is about to discuss a personalized and unique maintenance program for the women.

Dani and her comrades have been spending long hours in the training center. Sometimes Dani felt like there wasn't anything she couldn't do. She had never felt so strong, so powerful, so agile. She could run ten feet up the side of a wall and jump six feet into the air effortlessly.

The time came for combat training. It wasn't easy pretending to be a novice. To keep Jane Russell alive and protect her identity, she watched the other woman and at times copied their inexperienced moves. She had made friends with Kelly, Sandra and Becky. She was pretty certain she could trust them. Marcie was questionable. Gracie and Marcie seemed to get along real well.

As for Gracie, tension continued to build between the two of them. Gracie liked to win. She seemed to need to be the "leader" of the team.

As far as Dani was concerned, Gracie was the most dangerous of the women, mainly because of her attitude. She was tough and angry, guarded and full of resentment. With the street-smarts of a veteran hard-core alley cat, Gracie was unique. Dani knew if or when she had to bring out her real side, Gracie would be her first and biggest challenge. *Somehow I have to get Gracie on my side. I've got to get her to trust me.*

Sergeant Major John Madson shouted instructions as the women worked through their warm-ups, which for most anyone, would have been an overload workout.

Although Madson was tough on them and expected perfection, Dani liked him. If there ever was a superhuman, this man was he, yet she didn't feel threatened by him.

The Sgt. Major walked back and forth among them, observing their moves, demanding perfection. "You're going to have to do a lot better than this, ladies, life is about to get much tougher," he promised.

To Dani's chagrin, for the next two hours of training, she was partnered with Gracie. The tension between them increased as they work their combat exercises. Wanting to keep things from escalating, Dani said, "Not the time or the place, Gracie."

And Gracie responded with, "Maybe not today, but that day's a comin'."

Dani knew she was right.

SCENE 22

MISSION IMPOSSIBLE LAUNCHED

The day after the discussion at Starbucks.

Jason is sitting in the pilot seat of a rebuilt 70's Baron 58 twin Beechcraft. He straps himself in as Jack climbs in next to Jason. Bentley springs into the back seat beside Valentina, who already occupies the seat behind Jason. The engines howl.

The day before, after making rescue plans with Jason and Valentina, Jack notified the Chief of their plans.

The Chief tried to get Jack to hold off for a day, reasoning he would contact mercenaries Clay, Mack, Billy, Pete, Cam and J.D., and they could go together.

Jack insisted on leaving right away and would call the chief when he had more info.

Back at Seattle's N. Precinct W22, Chief Copper is briefing mercenaries Clay, Mac, Billy, Pete, Cam and J.D., regarding what they've tagged as Mission "Free Dani." The men are all seasoned veterans and fellow military comrades who fought side-by-side in the Vietnam War in the '70s.

"Comrades, we are headed toward an unknown base about which we have no intel yet. Jack contacted me; told me he has new information and was following the trail. That's why I've called you in. He's going on a hunch and a dream. Yes, a dream. I know, it doesn't sound like much to go on, but you know Jack. How often has he been wrong?

"As we speak, Jason, our Starbucks boy, witness #1, is piloting his daddy's restored, 70's Beechcraft, with permission, I must add; with his passengers Jack, Bentley and Valentina, our Starbucks witness #2. They left two hours ago. They've got a few hours on us and will assess the situation – be our eyes and ears on the ground."

"When Jack puts his mind to something, it's best to listen up," one of the men said.

The Chief nodded and proceeded to brief the men.

"That's all I got. Now, we need to move. We'll go over the strategy during the flight. Jack expressed his overwhelming gratitude for backing him up and at such short notice. And for backing him on a dream and a hunch, I might add."

"Wouldn't have it any other way," The men responded. "Semper Fi."

"I've contacted a friend in the Canadian military, and they have a private Sikorsky Sea King helicopter under contract with two pilots that will be waiting for us in Aklavik."

Sometime later, a Cessna Citation carrying nine men left the tarmac for Aklavik.

Jack placed a map and the flight plans in his lap. In case radio communication was lost, they were prepared.

An over-enthusiastic Bentley wiggled his way next to Valentina and stuck his head between the two front seats.

"Just like old times riding the patrol car, heh buddy."

Bentley barked.

"So this is your dad's twin-engine, you say?" Jack queried.

"A-hah," Jason answered, fiddling with the control system.

"And we have his permission...??"

"A-hah."

"And he taught you to fly?"

"He did," Jason responded, still concentrating on his flight setup.

"You're dad rebuilt this machine, did he?"

"Not really. I did most of it."

"OK. Now I am impressed. I don't impress easily. Whose idea was it to get landing skis for this plane? How often do you fly into snowy terrain?"

"My dad thinks of everything. He loves flying into the winter wilderness to photograph the solitude and wildlife. I tag along with him as often as I can."

"So that would be the reason it's now a four-seater vs six-seater. He needs the extra space for his photography equipment."

"You got it." Jason smiled a satisfied smile. He sensed Jack's approval. For some reason, that was important to him.

"You know, this beauty of a Beechcraft is Teflon coated," Jason added.

"Excellent and impressive. You and your dad did think of everything, didn't you," Jack commented.

"Why is this important?" Valentina asked.

"Because the Teflon coating will keep ice from sticking to the plane, and equally important, will help us evade radar detection," Jack answered.

"That's comforting. I just thought Teflon was used for pans."

"Teflon was initially invented for space shuttles and such."

"I do learn something new every day."

"Flight plans filed? Engines' been checked? All that sort of stuff?" Jack changed the topic.

"We're good to go," Jason answered.

"How's the fuel? Not that I need to ask."

"Topped up. With the enlarged fuel tanks in this baby, we will make it to Aklavik non-stop in about seven hours."

"Well then, I guess we are good to go. You got a name for this, "baby" of yours?"

"Course I do. Willow. Named after my twin sister."

"I didn't know you have a twin," Valentina interjected.

"I did have a twin. I lost my little sister when we were just kids. A freak kind of accident."

"Oh, I'm sooo sorry, Jason," Valentina said. "This plane, what a beautiful tribute."

"Thanks. It's like I have her with me when I'm flying. She was quite the prankster and adventurous one, so it's pretty fitting."

"Jason, I think your parents must be very proud of you," Jack said. *This young man is a breed of his own. I like this guy.*

Jason pulled started the engine. He went through his pre-flight check on a clipboard. When complete, he released the brakes, increased the throttle, and the plane inched forward. A few minutes later, the Beechcraft raced down the runway and lifted off, heading north and into a clear, blue sky.

Bentley whined. His ears perked forward intently as he focused on the radio.

"He's listening for familiar codes," Jack explained. "He's back in his element, that's for certain."

"You've got quite a partner there," Jason commented. "Saved your life and all, then lived to tell about it. Some dog you are, Bentley."

Bentley agreed.

SCENE 23

EXPOSED & CONFRONTED

After a long day of training followed by downtime and a meal, Dani, Kelly, Becky and Sandra chat as they walk down the long hallway that will take them to their sleeping quarters. Their chatter, accompanied by laughter. They are having one of the few lighter moments of the day.

"Want to know what I'd like?" Kelly didn't wait for a reply. "I'd kinda like to meet my old ex in a back alley—show him a trick or two."

Chuckles followed.

"I don't think that would be very fair," Dani commented, making a fake attack on Kelly.

"That's just what makes it so compelling," Kelly answered, counter-attacking.

"Speaking of tricks," Sandra the redeemed prostitute piped in, "I would like having it out with a few Johns myself. Let's see—there's Johnny Ice Man and then..."

"Ohh yeah, now that's a thought," Becky commented. "And you, Russell, who'd you like to square it off with? "Gotta be somebody."

"Na, nobody really," Dani answered. "Revenge is not my style."

"You can be such a badass, and then other times you're this little miss goody-two-shoes. It's like you don't know how to be mean—and yet you got no problem taking down. I like partnering with you."

Dani smiled and shrugged her shoulders.

Dani felt somewhat uncomfortable living the life of Jane. She wasn't uncomfortable being Jane; she was uncomfortable with how easy it had become to be someone she had to create on a daily basis. She was living the lie rather well, and she even surprised herself with how easy it was to be Jane. How long would this go on? Would she always have to be Jane Russell? Was she losing Dani?

Gracie and Marcie entered the hall and walked towards Dani and her companions. Dani immediately felt the tension rise inside her, and she flipped on her internal alert switch.

Something's not right. Casually Dani stepped aside to let the two women pass—they passed without a word—she relaxed. *Did I misjudge the intent?*

Kelly, Becky and Sandra, oblivious to everything except their silly banter, were still laughing and talking about whom else they'd like to administer attitude adjustments to when Dani spun around just in time to redirect Gracie, who was in full swing, attempting to blindside her.

Dani's auto-response kicked in, and she slammed Gracie into the wall. Gracie looked momentarily surprised; she had not expected that! A moment later, her anger-fueled, Gracie lunged at Dani with the vehemence of a vicious grizzly bear.

Besides their recent combat training, Gracie's street skills and smarts were something with which to reckon. Dani saw a switchblade slide out of Gracie's shirt sleeve and heard a click as she flicked the blade opened. Dani's response was involuntary—having the speed and preciseness of the trained fighter she was, she counter-attacked with equal fierceness.

Kelly, Becky, Sandra and Marcie froze.

Gracie's handling that knife much too well. Dani observed that Gracie held the knife loosely, the blade in her palm, flipping it from hand to hand, sure of her moves, her abilities. It was as if the knife was a part of her, a friend even.

This woman is determined, focused, waiting patiently for her opportunity. But I can take her. I've trained for this. She knows street fighting; I know a whole lot more. I've got this.

"We don't have to do this," Dani said calmly. "I'm not interested in fighting with you, Gracie. We could be friends, you and I— you know that."

The two circled.

"Friends? You and I? Hardly. And who are you anyway? Definitely not some Jane Russell. You don't got no signs like the rest of us got. You never been a user. We can't trust you. No—I don't think we'll be be'n friends you and I, anytime soon."

Dani realized why Gracie was out to get her. She was the enemy. Gracie knew she wasn't one of them. Would she have to give up Jane Russell? And at what expense? Dani would soon find out what it would cost her to become her real self once again. As things stood at that moment, she knew she had no other choice.

The two women shifted side to side, cat-like, watching each other's every move, muscles tensed and ready to defend.

Then Gracie closed in on Dani. Dani side-stepped, grabbed the knife in one lightening-smooth motion. In an instant, she had Gracie flat on her back with the knife at Gracie's jugular.

The room froze. No one spoke. No one even dared to move. Dani flipped the switchblade, snapping it shut. "OK, Gracie, you win. You're right. I owe you all an explanation."

"Come on, Jane, you don't owe the traitor a thing," Kelly piped up, having gathered her wits about her.

"Yeah, nothing," Becky and Sandra mimicked.

Marcie looked confused and didn't offer an opinion. She didn't know what to think, whose side to take. In fact, she didn't want to take sides. This wasn't her fight, but then again, it might soon have to be.

Dani stepped back and reached out her hand. "Get up."

Gracie ignored the hand and, with deft agility, sprung to her feet. Then Dani did the unexpected. "Here. You'll be needing this." She handed the closed knife to Gracie. "You're pretty darn good with that, and I'd rather be on your side than not. Come on, take it. Where'd you get that in here anyway?"

Gracie looked stunned, even befuddled. Slowly, tentatively she took the knife, then quickly slipped it up her sleeve. "I got ways," she answered. "So, go ahead—what's your story? You've got my attention."

Dani had no time to answer. The double doors at either end of the hall swung open and armed guards moved in swiftly and decisively; like a swarm of angry bees, they surrounded the women. Three guards strategically isolated Gracie and encouraged her to come with them—or get the taser treatment.

Gracie chose to submit without resistance, but before she disappeared behind the double doors, she turned to Dani.

"We're good," Dani reassured her. We're good. We'll fix this. I won't let you take the hit."

"What was that all about?" Marcie demanded. Marcie was a feisty fighter and was in the process of becoming an excellent operative. But in the world of espionage, she had a weak side. She did not like to have to choose sides. In her mind, things were either white or black. Plain and simple.

Naturally, Marcie got frustrated when things weren't white or black. That meant she had to make a decision not based on white or black, and she found that difficult to do.

Dani had figured Marcie out a long time ago—just like she had everyone else in her immediate sphere of influence figured out. "Marcie, you don't have to choose between us. It's OK. You heard—we're good. Sometimes we just have to work out some details—like any other family. There are always going to be disagreements. Right?"

Marcie nodded. When she heard Dani refer to them as a "family," her eyes watered up just a smidgen, and her heart missed several beats. Family was all she ever wanted, and now it seemed she had one. At least Dani said so, and from what she just witnessed, she decided she could trust Dani.

"What's going on? Where are you taking Gracie?" Sandra demanded.

"This is our matter. We don't need you messing in our business," Kelly added.

Disapproval was unanimous among the women.

"Orders," came one explanation from a guard with a smirk on his face. "Can't get away with too much around here."

"Off to the principal's office, all of you."

"Right this way," said another.

It was interesting to note; although heavily armed, the guards gave the "combatants" a wide, respectful berth.

SCENE 24

WHO CAN YOU TRUST?

Dani, Kelly, Sandra, Becky and Marcie are sitting on metal chairs, lined in a row against a cement wall. The secured and sound-proof room is located next to Dr. Frankel's office. The door unlocks and opens. In walks their instructor, Sergeant Major Madson. He stops and stands directly in front of the five women, his arms crossed, feet widespread, expressionless and saying nothing.

After several minutes, Dani stood to her feet, the others boldly follow. "Sir," Dani began.

The instructor shifted his gaze slowly to face Dani.

"Sir," she continued, "I would like to say something on behalf of Gracie."

"I'm not the one to negotiate with. My advice—keep quiet," was his curt response.

"She's—I—we—well—," Dani ignored his comment and hoped that other ears were listening. "Please. We need Gracie. This team needs her. I'm pretty confident we've settled our differences. What I'm saying is this mess we're in was just as much my fault as hers.

"I would like to see her have a second chance. I know she'll be good for it, and I'm sure I speak for the rest of us." Dani glanced questioningly at the other women looking for their positive responses. She breathed a sigh of relief as they all nodded in agreement.

"As I said, this is not my call."

The door opened, and Dr. Frankel walked into the room. "I'll take it from here, Sergeant Major." The Sergeant stepped aside.

"Jane, my office," the Dr. ordered.

As Dani followed the Dr., she turned to her comrades and mouthed, "I'll be back."

SCENE 25

SPY OR DIE MOMENT

In the privacy of his office, Dr. Frankel paces the room stopping every few seconds to glare at Dani, eyes on fire. He resumes his pacing. Dani stands quietly, waiting. Although uncertain as to what to expect, she remains calm and collected.

"So—looks like we've got ourselves a big problem," Dr. Frankel began.

"Yes, it does look like that, I know, but we got things sorted out. We're good. It had to come to this with Gracie; you know that."

"The problem goes much deeper than just your and Gracie's little power struggle."

Dani hesitated before saying, "You know the others know about me, don't you?"

"I do. Our little secret is not a secret any longer."

"So everyone knows then?"

"As far as I know, not everyone. I've been monitoring your activities.

"The other monitors I redirected. I sometimes do that—for your own protection, and mine. The guards were simply following my orders based on your little skirmish. I've altered the recording and removed anything about implicating you as not being Jane Russell. Thing is, Jane, Bacardi has spies everywhere.

"Sergeant Major, he knows," the Dr. continued. "I told him. He needs to know because he's my right-hand man, and I trust him. And he's indebted to me. If things get weird in the next few hours, we need him informed and on **our** side."

"Good. I knew we could trust the Sergeant Major. So I can assume no one is listening in on our conversation right now."

"That's right; I've got that taken care of. We can speak freely here. Dani, I don't want to lose you, lose any of my operatives, but what am I supposed to do?"

The Dr.'s agitation showed as he anxiously paced the room. "And now this. Inspection date is just three days away—this is not supposed to happen—not supposed to happen. How did I ever get mixed up in all this? If I could just live a normal life just once. That would be real nice, you know." Dr. Frankel punched the wall.

"I wouldn't be so sure," Dani said.

"Oh, I think normal would be..."

"I meant, Dr. Frankel..."

"Kurt, my name is Kurt. Can you just call me Kurt, please?"

"Kurt," Dani continued. "Um, Kurt, I meant I wouldn't be so sure that your days are numbered just yet. I do have a suggestion, a possible solution—one that you can live with, I think." Dani paused to let the thought sink in."

"Umm. You actually have a plan? I should know you would have a plan. OK, a plan would be good about now."

"Let me first get this straight," Dani said. "Are you saying that this somewhat insignificant incident means 'death to the project' and death to me, you, the other women?"

"Insignificant!? Insignificant!! This project has zero-tolerance for error. We aren't dealing with some, some—these people—they're not human."

"If we can't keep this between us, that means death. Yes, death to the project and death to you and the Sergeant Major—everyone, staff, they're all dispensable. Yes, they will also be terminated. The complete project." Dr. Frankel sighed in response. "They might spare mine because they need me, but I have no guarantees. I could soon be as dead as the rest of you all."

"That's pretty surreal, OK, let's say we have it coming," Dani said. "You know your way out of here; you've still got the controls to this whole thing. We can buy some time anyway. Let's do an inventory of the people we can count on.

"You can bet the women, including Gracie, are siding with me, and they're a force to be reckoned with, thanks to you and your scientific genius. Plus, we can count on Madson. My husband, Jack, will have ex-military people ready to assist him if he puts in a call. They can be here in about seven hours if we put in a call."

"We're going to need more than the eight of us and your husband's buddies to take these villains down."

"I heard you. But we have nothing to lose if what you say is true. You must have a burner phone here somewhere."

The Dr. unlocked a steel cabinet and handed Dani a phone.

"Details. Where are we? The coordinates – longitude and latitude?"

SCENE 26

FOLLOWING THE 'DREAM'

Jack's cell phone rings persistently, but the noise of the piston engines drowns out the sound. Bentley, however, like all dogs, endowed with super hearing powers, can hear the ringing. He tries to alert Jack by putting his nose into his master's jacket pocket.

"This isn't the time for snacks, buddy, and stop drooling on my jacket."

"Come on, Jack... pick up. Pick up the phone. Pleeeease... pick up."

Insistent on getting Jack's attention, Bentley barked two inches from Jack's face, spit flying everywhere. "Heh, what's up, buddy?" Jack whipped the spittle from his face. Again, Bentley dug his nose into Jack's jacket pocket, and this time, Jack realized this wasn't about snacks. "My phone is ringing! Thanks, buddy."

"Hello. Hello." Jack snapped to attention when he heard Dani's voice on the other end of the line. No small talk, no-nonsense, simply giving explicit instructions as to the facility's location where she and the others were imprisoned.

"What are the chances?!" he exclaimed! "It's Dani."

"YES!" Jason shouted, and Willow took an unexpected nosedive. With ease, he quickly recovered the craft, and they swooped smoothly over the tip of a white-capped mountain peak.

Jack grabbed Jason's clipboard and began to scribble down everything Dani was saying.

Our location: Latitude 68 degrees North, 31 minutes, 4 seconds Longitude 133 degrees West, 38 minutes, 29 seconds

"Dani, we're in the air as we speak, heading directly towards Aklavik. Guys, (Jack turned to his flight companions) we're on track. You were right, Valentina."

Valentina's stuck her head above Bentley's, not wanting to miss a thing.

"Who are you talking to?" Dani asked. "You're heading this way? How do you know where to look?"

"We had a God kind-of-sign, you could say— Valentina had a dream actually."

"A dream!? Valentina? How's that a sign?"

"Yes, a dream, and you'll just have to take my word for it right now. In this dream, she — listen, we can talk all about that later. We have nothing to lose, so we decided to take the dream as a sign."

'Apparently, we are less than two hours south of Aklavik."

"Who's we?"

"Bentley, uhh, Jason and Valentina from the coffee shop."

"Seriously? OK, that's good—I guess. That's good; we don't have much time."

"What are they? Oh, never mind. Once the Controllers realize we have a glitch, namely ME—the project will be terminated with extreme prejudice along with everyone in it."

"We won't let that happen to you or any of the other women, Dani," Jack said confidently, then asked, "The Controllers? Terminated?"

"Right now I'm here with the project manager genius who's in charge of this operation. His life is on the line too, and we've got to get ourselves out of this place ASAP."

"I hear you."

"Listen, Jack—some things have changed. I'm not the same Dani, you know. I'm a highly-trained operative; a hostile one, of course. No joke."

"This just gets better all the time," Jack yelled into the phone. "Did you say operative? Listen, Chief Copper and some of my other marine buddies are lined up for backup. We'll have you all out of there by the end of the day." (pause). "Do you copy, Dani."

"Copy that. Great news, Jack. Now, you need to know one other very important little detail."

"What's that?"

"I don't look at all like myself. I've kinda had the ultimate makeover."

"OK—I can live with that!" Jack answered. "Good or bad? Don't answer cause it doesn't matter. I love you either way."

"Not at all like myself, Jack; keep that in mind."

"Remember our code word? The one you gave me on the plane?" He continued.

"I remember."

"You know what you've got to do—we'll be there as soon as possible. Check in with me when you can. By the way, the Chief is right behind us in a Citation, and he's arranged for a Sea King helicopter to take us from Aklavik to the base. Over and out."

"So we've got reception out here. That's interesting," Valentina said.

"It's a satellite cell phone, is why," Jason answered.

"I've been too many places and seen too many things to not be prepared," Jack answered.

"Once a Navy Seal, always a Navy Seal, heh?"

"Right now, I couldn't be more thankful for my years as a Seal."

SCENE 27

NOW WHAT?

Dani returns the phone and takes a deep breath, the expression on her face priceless.

"Would you believe it! They're less than two hours away!" Dani announced. "And his mercenary buddies aren't far behind. Things are starting to look good. I'm going to need the layout of this place; floor plans, security details, that sort of stuff. I also need to know who tells YOU what to do, Dr. Frankel—Kurt. Who's your boss?"

"Wow, that was fast. How did they? Right, never mind. His name is Bacardi. I report to him weekly— he makes unexpected visits and reports to somebody in Washington. No idea who, just know he's not your regular kind of guy."

"Bacardi. A bottle of premium rum, no less. So what do you know about him? Anything, everything."

"His real name, no idea. He won't have any problem terminating any of us personally. No man can beat him in a fight— that I know of. He's evil, pure evil. I've seen evil-looking through his steely eyes, right through me, paralyzing. I think he's the devil personified."

"Good to know— we'll be ready for him then," Dani answered confidently.

"Seriously? Who are you anyway? I'll have you know that man is terrifying." Beads of sweat had begun to form on the Dr.'s forehead. "I know you've gained some remarkable superpowers, but this guy isn't all about physical strength. He's not even human. Do you hear what I'm saying?

"Dani, this guy is no human. I'm not easily—what I'm telling you is—this guy is not just some billionaire technologist – he's like a demon inside of a billionaire technologist body, and he is terrifying. It's this paralyzing power he carries inside him, around him, it's hard to explain."

"OK. That explains a few things," Dani responded. I hear you loud and clear, Kurt. I know what you mean. But you are going to have to pull yourself together. It's not who we are or who he is that counts. Who's on our side—that's what counts. You say he's the devil himself? Well, that tells me a lot about the enemy, and that also tells me he can be beaten. Do you hear what I'm saying?"

"I hear what you're saying alright, you just never met this kind of enemy."

"Maybe so, but I sure have met the devil. And if you believe there is a devil, you most certainly must believe there is a God. The God I serve has this devil beat, hands down."

"When you put it that way. So you're one of those 'Christ-followers'?"

"I am. You have a problem with that?"

"Ahh—no, I don't think so. Maybe if I'd known this about you when we first met, I'd have a problem with that, but not now, not after watching you in action. This explains a lot of things.

"You've got substance and inner strength like I haven't seen in anyone, ever. You're fearless, and if you do have fear, you sure don't show it."

"Kurt. I battle fear, like everyone else, but my relationship with God is the reason I can beat it. Look, we can have more of this conversation once we're all safely out of here. In the meantime, remember you can talk to God yourself. You understand all about creating, inventing stuff. God is the ultimate creator, and you're one of his creations. He doesn't take lightly to the devil messing with his creation. That is how God feels about you.

"Kurt, nothing happens without a reason. There's always a bigger picture. For example, it's no mistake I was mistaken for Jane Russell. I'm here for a reason, and I met you for a reason, which as far as I'm concerned to let you know God is real and there for you."

"Well, that stuff is all good for you, but I don't see how having God in my life is going to work for me."

"Just think about what I said. Now we've got to get on with the plan. We don't have a lot of time to waste. We can pick up this conversation later, I promise."

"Let's hope we have a later."

"I need to go talk to the others," Dani said. "Fill them in on things. I'm sure they must be sweating it out, wondering what's going on."

"Wait, we can't take the others," Kurt cautioned, a warning look in his eye. "We'll never make it out of here alive if we try and save everybody!"

"Kurt, as far as I'm concerned, it's all or none of us. I don't compromise. And what about your right-hand man, the Sergeant? You're going to abandon him and jump ship without him?"

"You're right. What was I thinking? I'm not thinking."

"I would never do that. That's not me," the Dr continued.

"No, that is not you. And what about the Sergeant Major? You are certain we can trust him?"

"Absolutely. He's not here by choice. He'd like nothing better than to get out of this assignment. And, I can trust him with my life. He's always got my back."

Dani looked out the office window at the Major. "Good, because I've got a good feeling about him. OK, first things first. We've got to rescue Gracie. Where is she?

"Level 4—isolation unit."

The Dr. turned to his computer and started typing. I'm resetting the access code right now—to her cell unit. I know where she is at all times. This little device here (the Dr. showed Dani a little black quarter-sized item, a tiny red light flashing) one of a kind virtual tracking device, lets me know where she is at all times. It's all tied into a Global Positional System - GPS tracking."

"Really. GPS tracking?"

"Yep, but significantly more accurate and sophisticated than anything you might be familiar with."

"So, how does it track Gracie?"

"A tiny chip. In her tattoo. I planted a chip."

"So you can track every one of us? Know where we are at any given time?"

"I can. You think I don't know what you all are up to pretty much every minute of the day? But not to worry. I have not reported this to headquarters yet. This was a little experiment of mine which I needed to make sure was working as expected."

"You invented this thing, when?"

"1957."

Note: According to Wikipedia, the inventor of the GPS device is unknown.

> "Well, finding the inventor of GPS device is a very tough task…it's a debatable topic…the inventor of GPS device, whoever she/he may be is lying in the dark side of history…."
> **https://www.quora.com/Who-invented-the-GPS-tracking-device**

"That's way before—OK, too much information for me to process right now. But I guarantee you when this is all over, that chip comes out." Dani pointed to the tattoo on her shoulder.

"I'll be happy to do that for you."

"Not sure I want you to be touching me ever again."

"You don't want the wrong people to know about this, do you?"

"Right. Maybe I'll do it myself."

"When this is all over—you and me—any chance?" Kurt asked, hopefully.

Dani glared at the Dr.

The responding look on his face was a sheepish one. But, not one to give up easily, he replied, "Right. But you're not the same woman, are you? How's he going to feel about that?"

Dani gave Kurt another look of warning.

Kurt quickly added, "I want you to know I'm there for you; that's all."

Dani moved to leave. Kurt stopped her, put his hand on her arm, then asked, "How old am I?" The Dr. laughed nervously.

"I have no idea," she answered. "After what you just told me, I have no idea whatsoever." *What's with the triviality?* "Why do we care about that now?"

"I turn ninety-three on Thursday."

"Ninety-three!" Dani exclaimed, her eyes wide, mouth open in surprise.

"Pretty impressive, heh?"

"Well, Dr. Frankel, you had **me** fooled, that's for sure. Course I should have guessed you would take advantage of the project. Why wouldn't you? But ninety-three.!! I never thought about how this technology of yours has the power to gain you a lifetime! Or more! I can see why you love this part of the project."

"As you rightfully said, 'THIS part of the project.' It would be remiss of me NOT to take advantage of the revolutionary rejuvenation technology I've developed, wouldn't it? That's what a good scientist does; we test our theories on ourselves if it's possible."

"Of course. I understand that. But we can discuss this all later."

"I don't think you understand. You're confusing me with all this God stuff and how interested He's supposed to be in me. I've got a lot of questions, you know. And I've got other things to think about right now. This isn't easy— leaving my precious lifeblood behind, for one."

"Great! Seriously! Did you say precious? I can see why you might have difficulty letting God have a say in things; you just might have to give up your precious lifeblood."

"See, you don't understand. You are mocking me."

"Look— maybe I don't understand, but I do know you can leave all this behind. We all have to die one day or another. And when we do die, we can know for certain where we're going once our time on earth is done.

"Dr. Frankel, you've got the rest of us beat by fifty, sixty years or more. Come on, old man," she added with a smirk. "Look at it this way; you've bought yourself a whole new lifetime. You've still got a lot of living to do, and so do the rest of us."

Dani gently released the Dr.'s firm grasp on her arm. "We're going to do this. Just remember what we talked about and keep your wits about you. So, are you ready to go or do I have to make you?"

"The Dr. grabbed a brown leather bag, stuffed some papers into it. He went to a hidden safe, opened it and took out several floppy disks. He stood tall and looked Dani in the eye. "I'm good to go."

"OK, let's do this." The Dr. opened the door. Dani walked over to Sergeant Major Madson and the four women operatives.

"Here's the plan…"

SCENE 28

MISSION FREE DANI

The Chief and men are resting as the Citation heads northward. The Chief's phone rings; Jack is on the other end.

"Listen up, men. That was Jack. We have more intel," the Chief announced. "This is the latest. Dani made contact with Jack just minutes ago. The good news is, she is still very much alive. She was able to give Jack the coordinates of the facility where she and the other hostages are being held.

"We've learned this facility is used solely to train selected, chosen women to become covert operatives. They are trained and have their appearance altered and their physical abilities enhanced to a level that supersedes anything I've ever heard of.

"We are out-numbered, from the information Dani gave, but we do have the element of surprise for the time being. The bad news is, time is of the essence. As good as Jack is, he can't do this on his own.

"A guy by the name of Dr. Kurt Frankel is in charge of the project at the facility. As his life may very likely also be on the line, he is on board with 'Mission Free Dani.'

"He was there when Dani made the call. Once their headquarters gets word that Dani is not Jane Russell, all hell is going to break loose.

"The project has zero error tolerance. Now that Dani's true identity has come to light—the operation is scheduled for termination. Those on the immediate list for termination: our six women operatives and trainer, Sergeant Major Madson. We suspect that everyone is targeted for termination, but we can't be certain at this point. Dr. Frankel, he might be too valuable an asset to be terminated.

"The facility has state-of-the-art security as well as armed security guards and 4 or 5 K9s. The camouflaged outer structure blends into the landscape so it won't be easy to locate, not even by air.

"At this point, we have the element of surprise. We've got six highly trained operatives and the Sergeant Major as assets. As for the Dr., he is our access man, and we need him if we're going to get those women out of there.

"That's our mission, men. Jack and the team will be at the base in less than two hours. They'll scope the area on foot, locate the facility and wait for us to join them.

"Any questions so far?"

"What's their escape plan?" Clay asked. "And how does one of our key witnesses, Valentina Juarez, factor into all this?"

"The facility has six levels. Our hostages are housed on the 2nd floor. They train on the 1st floor, and medical facilities are on the 3rd floor. The 4th floor is interrogation and detention. The other floors are storage. The escape plan calls for our targets to get to the roof.

"According to Jack, Valentina has cat burglary skills, of all things, under her belt. Not sure what that's all about, but Jack knows what he's doing, and at this point, we don't need the details.

"She'll scale the wall and assist our hostages down from the roof six floors up. The operatives should be waiting for Valentina and the rappelling gear Jack acquired. Jack is our sniper man and Jason, our eyes and ears."

"Well, as we've said before, we know Jack knows what he's doing," Billy said.

"I think this might be one of the craziest missions we've ever taken on," Clay said. "But, we've got this."

SCENE 29

THE PLAN

Dr. Frankel, Dani and her comrades watch intently over the Dr.'s shoulder as he alters the women's records on the computer. He alters personal information as well as cellular records and charts. All video recordings and digital images of the women's new physical appearances are also altered. The major stands guard.

"Amazing!" Kelly commented.

"It's the software. I developed it so no one will be the wiser."

"I'm impressed," Sandra said. "Now, at least we'll have half a chance out there."

"You're a good man, Dr. Frankel. You're doing the right thing," Dani added.

"I hope so. I feel like I'm going to need redemption after all this is over. Something I would never have felt before I met you, by the way. That's rather disturbing, you know."

"Disturbing in a good way," Dani responded.

"I suppose. Maybe—I hope so. But not so sure about that." Dr. Frankel pulled up the floor plans on the computer. The plans showed the building with six stories. "Here's our best escape route. The top floors are either empty or used for storage.

"Access is restricted. All exits/entrances are guarded—dogs are everywhere; access codes are constantly changing at every entrance and exit, some thermal sensors and specific to restricted personnel. I've overridden the codes, but they probably won't be any good for much longer. The Dr. pointed out the route to the top floor and onto the roof. If your rescue team gets here as expected, we just might have a chance. But first, we've got to get past the gauntlet without the guards getting a scent something's gone amiss."

"Your plan will have to work then. I need to call Jack; give him the latest lowdown."

The Dr. handed her the burner phone. After a quick update with Jack, Dani handed the phone back to him.

"Remember, Bacardi could be notified at any moment something is wrong, and once he does, everything shuts down. Then it's shoot-to-kill," Dr. Frankel added. "This is not going to be easy, in fact, I still say pretty much impossible."

"Nothing is impossible. As for the dogs, leave them to me. Let's let Jack and his team work out the rest of the details for us, OK. That's his specialty."

"Really," the Dr. asked, hope in his voice.

"Really."

"Just how special?"

"Navy Seal special. And inside intelligence information beyond my knowledge."

The Dr. took a deep breath and let it out. "Best get on with it then."

"I'll hang back—if all hell breaks loose, I can take care of things from this end," the sergeant said.

"No. We need you. And I certainly don't want to lose you. You've been the only one I could trust in this place."

"OK. Then I'll be your inside man, Kurt."

"He's right, Kurt," Dani interjected. "We need an inside man. No one will suspect him. The sergeant can take care of himself. If you think us women are imposing—I need say no more."

"True," Kurt replied. "Course having had something to do with that—I do know what you are capable of, Sergeant Major. I do see the wisdom of an inside man, one such as yourself. Wait! The code to the safety chamber. You may need it. 007 288 247. Got that?"

"Got it."

"What's the safety chamber?" Dani inquired.

"If all is lost, one might just survive the coming blast if we are inside the chamber. It's never been tested, but I did build it for that purpose. Self-preservation and all."

"Hopefully, I won't be the one to test it out," the sergeant said. "007288247."

"Wait," Dani interjected. "We have our rescue team out there, and they need to know you are a friendly. Here, take this." Dani ripped off the bottom of her outer shirt and tossed it to him. Use this as a bandana. It's got my scent."

The Major looked puzzled.

Then Dani reached over and ripped off the pocket of the Major's uniform. "This is for Bentley," she said.

"Seriously! Who's Bentley?" a confused Major asked.

"Bentley is a dog. Not your ordinary dog. He's a highly trained K9 officer who nobody wants to mess with. You do not want him thinking you are one of the bad dudes. When I get the chance, I'll use this to make sure he has your scent. And if you have my scent on you, all the better. Believe me; you'll thank me later."

"OK. I'm good with that. Bentley, I'll be watching for you," the Major said. "We'll see you all on the other side then."

"And, I'll let the team know to keep watch for you. Just don't lose that head wrap."

"All good," the Major answered.

Dani stuffed the ripped pocket inside her vest.

SCENE 30

SCOPING THE LANDSCAPE

Back in the Beechcraft, Jack, Jason and Valentina survey the white and frozen landscape for what could be the Spy or Die facility.

"According to Dani's information, we are close to our target," Jack commented.

"Looks pretty desolate to me," Jason said.

"To not be seen, you must learn from the chameleon," Valentina responded. "It's there somewhere— you just can't see it because it's made to look like all the rest of the landscape."

"You've got that right. Take her down, Jason. Need me to take over?"

"I've got this," Jason responded confidently.

As the plane glided through the air, Jason and Jack scanned for a place to land. "Looks like a good spot just to the left on that stretch right over here," Jack directed. "It almost looks like a landing strip. And it's almost exactly at the coordinates."

"Keep her steady, back, back..."

Jason reduced the throttle, set Willow down on her skis and brought the plane to a stop.

"OK! That was way too much fun," Valentina exclaimed, her knuckles white, still gripping the back sides of the pilot seat.

"You liked that, did you?" Jason laughed. He took in a deep breath. "You're my kind of passenger. Not a bad landing, considering all things, if I don't say so myself."

"That was well done," Jack agreed. "I don't think I could have done it better. Your dad taught you well."

"I'll take that as a compliment," Jason said, a big grin on his face. Thank you, sir."

"OK. Focus, team. Things are about to get rather delicate, if you know what I mean. And we don't have time to waste. We've got our GPS and coordinates. Jack checked his satellite phone. Our backup, Chief Copper and comrades just notified me, they are on their way."

"That is great news," Jason said.

Bentley jumped out of the plane and gave an enthusiastic bark. The three followed.

Jack bent down and took Bentley's head between his hands. "Bentley. We're heading into enemy territory, and from here on in, you will need to restrain yourself. That means this is a 'silent mission.' You got that, Bentley?"

Bentley shoved his nose into Jack's hand and gave a low rumble. He knew what was expected of him, and he was more than ready. His muscular body quivered with anticipation.

Jason opened the storage compartment and pulled out three large white duffle bags. They contained white thermal full-body outerwear, head-gear, eye ware, balaclavas, thermal gloves and boots; everything white like the snowfields surrounding them.

The party of four, even Bentley, were soon outfitted in camouflage, white, weather-proof, breathable, protective gear. Only Bentley's eyes, ears and mussel exposed. He was pretty pleased with his attire.

They covered the Beechcraft with a huge, white tarp that would decrease radar detection and visibility. The team distributed the weight among them—water packs, medic/survival kit, climbing gear and ropes.

Jack zipped opened the last duffle bag and pulled out a couple of Micro Uzis. He handed one to Valentina and one to Jason. "Take a moment and go over our training," Jack instructed. "In the heat of the action, you want to react the way you trained. I know we only had a couple of sessions. Only think about what you do know, not what you don't know. Got that?"

"Got that," they both answered. "Think about what we know."

He handed them each two more handguns and a six-inch, sheathed hunting knife."

"I'm not like you two," Jason said somberly. "Valentina – you said your dad taught you how to handle a gun when you were just a kid. You've both got way more experience with this stuff. Just over a week ago, I'd never even held a handgun. Let alone an Uzi. I sure hope I don't mess up."

"You won't. I got your back, son," Jack replied as he clapped Jason on the shoulder.

"If you can handle a plane like you did today, you can do this."

"If you say so, sir. I'll keep that in mind."

"See this gadget." Jack picked up a 2 x 1 inch rectangular box. "It detects infra-red motion detectors. Aim and push this here button, and you immobilize them."

'Cool. Where do you get access to this stuff?" Jason asked.

"Special Ops."

"Right."

"The facility is just over 200 yards N. E. from where we're standing. Depending on the conditions, we'll get there just before sunset. And that's a good thing because we can use the shadows to our advantage."

Bentley took the lead.

SCENE 31

BUSTED

Dani, Dr. Frankel and the other female operatives are walking down the long corridor leading to an elevator, which will take them to the fourth floor, detention/interrogation. They turn a corner and are confronted by two snarling rotties.

"I've got this," Dani said. "Just keep an eye out."

"We got your back," Becky assured her.

"Platz." Dani gave the "sit" command. Both dogs whine and hesitate, seemed confused. Dani used a hand command and looked the dogs right in the eye resulting in both dogs responding by moving slowly into a down-stay position.

"That was baller," someone said. (Slang for "cool" in the 2000's)

Taking a wide berth around the dogs, the escapees moved ahead and continued towards the elevator.

Rounding another corner, as expected, they met up with a security guard. A lackadaisical one, it appeared. Leaning against the wall, catching a standing snooze, having little to do but walk down empty halls and stare into empty rooms day after day, boredom set in, leaving him off his game for the moment. The snooze was light; his senses told him he was not alone—he jumped to attention, one hand on his holster, the other his taser.

"Stay calm, use your charm and smile, smile," Dani whispered.

Everyone smiled nonchalantly.

"We seem to be lost. So glad you're here. This place is endless—a maze," she began.

The guard relaxed and returned the smile until he saw Dr. Frankel. His smile melted. "Does the Dr. not know where he is?"

"I'm in need of some—working on the output program—we have some detail work that needs to be done. And we did get a little confused, yes, I'm not so good with directions, and my escort wasn't available. Could you please give us access to the 4th floor?"

"Your escort wasn't available. Surely someone was available?"

"My personal escort 006 wasn't available. This simply cannot wait. We're dealing with sensitive matters. This involves the, um, very safety of these women, so please, you have my orders."

"Yes, sir, I understand. But why the 4th floor?"

"Surely you would expect interrogation to be an integral part of the program."

"Of course, sir. I can escort you, but first, I need to make a call in and confirm our status. He reached for his radio…"

And then pandemonium set in. What happened next, happened in seconds—the women's reaction, the guard realizing he had been had, him reaching for his gun and the result—In less than a second, Dani had the guard disarmed. A skill Jack had taught her.

She slammed her left hand firmly on the pistol hammer, and with the other hand, twisted the hardware out of the guard's grip. A shot fired. Intentionally on Dani's part.

The bullet tore into the guard's left foot. He let out a yell and crumbled to the floor. Leaving the clip with the remainder of the bullets in the chamber, Dani tossed the ammunition to Gracie.

Dani turned her attention back to the injured guard. She ripped off the bottom half of Becky's shirt this time and wrapped the strip tightly around the wound. "Sorry about that. But you won't die on my account."

Dani dragged the guard and placed his right palm onto the ID plate. The door opens. Dani hesitated —then, with a quick pinch on the neck, put the guard to sleep. "Sorry," she said once again. "Really, I am."

They stepped into the spacious elevator.

That's when a myriad of Red lights began flashing.

"We've been busted!" Kelly declared. "We'll be trapped in this box! I do not like this one bit."

"We may be busted, but they don't know where we are," Dr. Frankel responded. "Remember, I said I would take care of the technical aspects. I did some fancy systems sabotaging." The Dr. grinned. "They won't be able to shut this elevator down for at least another 20 minutes. Our tech guy will need some time before he figures this out. I always have my personal rescue plan right up to date and operational within minutes. They'll be looking for us in all the wrong places."

"And that will buy us some valuable time," Dani answered. "Dr. Frankel, you can be so brilliant and yet, you can be so stupid."

"I suppose any compliment at this point is…"

A voice over the intercom interrupted, "Attention, this is only a drill. Everyone, please make your way in an orderly manner to Level One, Section 104N. Please proceed immediately to Level One, Section 104N. I repeat, this is only a drill."

"Maybe we're not busted. Maybe this is for real. And if we don't show up, they'll really know we're onto something," Marcie said.

"That was Head of Security," the Dr. stated.

"Yes, that was Head of Security," Becky affirmed.

"How do you know?" Dani asked. "I've never met the guy, or heard his voice, far as I remember."

"Several weeks ago, when I was going for my Level 4 assessment appointment, he was in Dr. Frankel's office and having the keen hearing that I do, thanks to Dr. Frankel, I overheard the last bit of their conversation. I never forget a voice."

"OK. So how do you know THAT voice was the Head of Security?"

"Heard the Dr. address him as such, plain and clear—he said, 'As Head of Security, I would appreciate your cooperation when it comes to... blah blah blah.'"

"So, Dr. Frankel, you passed another test," Dani looked at the Doctor, who shrugged and responded with, "I AM on your side."

Dani continued, "We know they're on to us and don't want to alarm us. They want us to show up, making things easy for them. Team, the fight is on."

"Bring it on then," Sandra responded. "We're as ready as we'll ever be, thanks to 'the program.'"

SCENE 32

ALL ABOUT GRACIE

The elevator doors slide open, and the troop enters a large open area that has a creepy kind of look to it—high ceilings, clammy cold and dimly lit. They see four sets of double doors - N. S. E. W. The Dr. leads them to set #1 labelled N—to his left.

"We're going to encounter plenty of security past these doors and several 100 meters to our right," he said.

"This place is endless. So, they won't be expecting us?"

"No, they will not. I've scrambled signals and activated neutral responses to inquiries. My techies won't be able to figure this out either for at least a couple of hours." The Dr. chuckled. He appeared quite pleased with his brilliant self. "Maybe they will never figure it out."

"Seems to me you know a lot more about all this technical stuff than Barcadi, knows you know."

"It's called artificial intelligence, Jane," the Dr. answered. "And, yes, I know more about artificial intelligence and the inevitable than 99.999% of the world—and that includes those financing and running this show. I'm hoping that's my life insurance policy."

"So, what kind of artificial intelligence exactly are you talking about? Never mind. We'll get to that when this is all over."

"Yes," the Dr. agreed. "Quiet everyone. We're going to encounter more security any time now."

Indeed, several hallways and corners later, the troop encountered several heavily armed but unsuspecting guards. Before they knew what was happening, they were disarmed and "asleep."

The women see their comrade, Gracie, locked in a steel bar cell in the middle of the spacious, otherwise barren room, a single metal chair some six feet from the enclosure. It contains a small military cot, military dark green blanket, washbasin and bottle of water; and an untouched orange in a paper plate on the floor by the cot.

"What took you so long?" Gracie peered through her prison bars, a serious look on her face. "And why the Dr.?"

Dani chuckled. "Good to see you too. Had a few things to work out, the Dr. and I, and he's with us. He's the reason we're here."

The Dr. stepped forward, typed in a series of numbers on a keypad, and the heavy cell door screeched open.

Gracie couldn't get out of the steel cage fast enough. "Much as I don't like owing nobody, I owe you plenty."

"As you can see, we're all in this together, and we got your back. So, let's get right to it. My real name is Dani, but until we get to safety, I'm Jane Russel. Got that?"

"Sure do. I never had someone got my back before. Like this, for real, I mean."

"Things are different. You got a whole team now got your back. Heh, no time to get sappy.

"We've got to move. Stick close; we're breaking out of this place."

"Nothin' I'd like better."

The women greeted Gracie, one by one, assuring her Dani spoke for them—that she was one of them.

"OK, Enough of this homecoming business," the Dr. stated. Let's get these bodies in the cage. That'll buy us some time. We've got to hurry it up."

The women tossed the sleeping guards into the cell. Dr. Frankel drew a tiny glass container from his pocket. He sprayed a shot of something under each of the subdued guard's noses and then secured the cell. "That'll keep them sleeping for hours."

"Nice trick," Sandra commented.

"Why do you all look so surprised. You haven't seen nothin' yet. OK, let's go," The Dr. ordered. "Move—this way. We're taking the stairs. They are just around the corner, and we'll need to make a stop on the fifth floor."

"Why the fifth floor stop?" Kelly asked.

"Supplies. We'll be needing supplies, and fifth floor's got it all."

SCENE 33

THE FACILITY

Jack, Jason and Valentina are snowshoeing across the white sea of snow towards a mountain of ice and snow they believe covers the facility. Dusk is settling in, and the shadows begin to play a new set of tricks.

"Our target is right here in front of us. Notice those sharp edges over on the far right. This is a man-made ice formation, and you can bet underneath it all is the Spy or Die facility."

"You mean that whole massive mountain of ice—that's huge."

"That's it, I'm sure," Jack said.

"Does look a little suspect," Jason commented. "Where's the entrance? How in the world do they get into this thing, and how do they breathe in there?"

"As Valentina said, it's all a camouflage. Fascinating as far as airflow, if you look over to the North, see that hint of steam and mist. That'll be your ventilation system right there.

"Looks like a mountain of ice letting off steam is all."

"This thing is gigantic. Like six stories high and three city blocks wide, I'd say. What all goes on in there?"

"We are about to find out." Jack looked at his watch. "In 15 minutes and 43 seconds, you are on Valentina. Are you ready?"

"Oh, I'm ready. This is one challenge I do not want to miss."

"That's what I like to hear."

Valentina headed for the wall.

SCENE 34

THE LIFE LINE

Back inside Operation Spy or Die, Dr. Frankel separates himself from the group of women, and without them noticing, slips into room 512.

"Dr., how much further till we get to the supply room? Dr. Frankel? Where is that man?"

As one, the women stopped, realizing the Dr. had eluded them.

"That crazy doctor. The traitor He's ditched us," Marcie said, her teeth clenched.

"I think I know what he's up to. Marcie, Gracie, help me check the rooms," Dani ordered. The rest of you keep us covered."

Moving quickly, the three ran back down the hallway, checking each room as they pass it. Dani found the Dr. in Room 512, frantically filling his deep pockets with little vials from a glass cupboard.

"Got him," Dani shouted to the others. She addressed the Dr. "What are you doing?" Dani didn't wait for an answer as she knew exactly what he was doing. "You can't take this stuff with you. You do **not** need this stuff."

"I must I must— I can't leave without my lifeblood, my life's work."

"Listen, listen, Dr. Kurt." Dani tried to reason. "You are a brilliant chemist, amongst countless other incredible things. You've done this once; you can do it again. You don't need this stuff."

But the Dr. would not relent. Dani grabbed him by his collar and dragged him unceremoniously out into the hallway. Dr. Frankel, all the while, continued to stuff whatever he could grab, into his pockets and the pockets of the lab coat. Although quite capable of holding his own physically, the Dr. was more concerned with protecting the vials."

The not-so-patient Gracie got right up close and personal and shook her finger in the doctor's face. "Get a grip, man. You'll cost us our lives, you idiot. Are you with us or not?"

"Course I'm with you. This is for your benefit too, I'll have you know. Maintenance is of utmost importance. Can you step back a little, a little more, more, please. And if you stop me, I don't know why I should cooperate. I'm not leaving without this. Remember, I built you and don't you think I didn't build myself as well."

Slowly, Gracie backed down while Dani released her grip on his collar. The Dr. straightened out his attire, a miffed look on his face. "OK, if this stuff gets in the way of our escape, I promise I will drop it like a hot potato."

"We don't have time for this nonsense. I'll hold you to that." Dani said. "According to your specs, we've got to be close to the stairwell that'll take us to the roof. Right?"

"Straight ahead, around the corner, through a set of double doors and to the right."

Dani checked the Dr.'s watch. "Jack and his team should be watching for us in ten minutes.

"Check your little GPS gadget you showed me earlier. Can we listen in on security's conversations?"

"No, Was in my plans, though."

"Worth a try. Let's move."

"Wait," the Dr. said. "Room 520— we'll need some ..."

"Oh no you don't," Sandra hissed.

The Dr. threw up his hands and replied with urgency in his voice. "People. We need winter gear. Coats! Warm stuff, if we're going to survive out there for more than a few minutes, you realize. And weapons. We need some of those."

The women shrugged and nodded, relieved the Dr. appeared to be in his right mind at the moment. In minutes they were outfitted and continued to make their way up the stairwell. Becky opened the door, and a cold blast of arctic air hit them full in the face. Dusk had settled in, and visibility was poor. One could not tell where the building ended or how far the drop was to the white snow below.

"Where are you, Jack?" Dani muttered. She pulled her balaclava up over her nose. "You can show up any minute now. You're close by; I know you're out there, Jack."

"What now? Where's this Jack of yours? Marcie cried, trying to be heard above the wind.

Dani looked to the North, the East, West and South. She saw a movement— something tossed onto the roof. *There's our life-line.* She moved towards it, motioning for the others to follow.

SCENE 35

YOU DON'T SPY
YOU DIE

Back on the main floor in the sound-proof conference room, the Head of Security is reporting via satellite to an irate and out-of-control Bacardi. He screams orders from the other side of a 75" screen.

"The Spy or Die initiative is terminated as of this second. From now on it's shoot to kill. Every bit of evidence must be eradicated. Not a trace of anyone or anything left when you leave the site. It appears our operatives have chosen to die. Is that understood?

"Completely understood, sir."

"I'm sending in a drone to finish the job. Spy or Die premises will soon be nothing but a cloud of smoke and a hole in the ground. You have about two hours to do your job. You will be notified on your com device when the drone is five minutes away. Find those rogue 20 million dollar operatives and put a bullet in all 6 of them.

"Don't think I'll make this easy for you. I repeat I want their bodies, in body bags, delivered to me personally. I hold you responsible for having those bodies out of the premises before it's torched. As for Dr. Frankel, I want him alive. Do I make myself clear?

"I am not done with him."

"Perfectly clear, sir. I'll have the planes prepared for take-off immediately."

"What's the status on your numbers?"

"Fifty-four, including myself. Eighteen men under my command, including three pilots and two aircraft personnel and mechanics. Dr. Frankel's technician, Michael Cross, special ops trainer, Sergeant Major John Madson, seven research assistants and twenty-two facilities auxiliary staff including kitchen and housecleaning."

"Terminate them all, except two pilots. I want the bodies of the six operatives back here—you know what to do. Clean up the mess. And I want Dr. Frankel alive."

Bacardi pushed a button, and the screen went blue.

Meanwhile, security members now turned assassins, found the disabled guard, along with several whining, disorientated K9s. The lead man shook the guard and yelled for him to "wake up." A few slaps got the desired effect. Slowly the guard regained consciousness. He opened his eyes—a circle of faces peering down at him. Confused, *What's happening?*—his first thought. The next moment he knew exactly where he was and what had transpired. Embarrassment and regret rushed over him. *How could I have been so taken? I had one job to do, and I failed.* Fear rushed in, quickly followed by resignation. *This is it. My days are over.*

The lead man fired questions at the injured guard. "What happened? What happened?"

"Dr. Frankel, and his operatives…"

"Which way did they go?"

"Fourth floor, sir."

"What did they want?"

Something to do with the program training, but…"

"Why are the dogs acting like idiots?"

"Operative Number Six, she—I swear, she put some kind of spell…"

"I've heard enough. Don't waste a bullet and risk announcing our whereabouts. Besides, this dirt bag's not going anywhere, and we're running out of time."

Resigned to his fate, the injured guard did not resist. He knew the protocol.

The heartless commandos left the injured guard along with the dogs to their imminent demise.

SCENE 36

THE GREAT ESCAPE

$\mathbf{A}$ grappling hook sinks deep into the ice wall. Valentina tugs the rope. Satisfied it is secure, she nimbly begins her climb. In less than ninety seconds she had scaled the ice wall and come face-to-face with Dani.

There was no time for greetings. Dani gave Valentina a quick nod of thanks and acknowledgement. Valentina acknowledged with a nod in return.

With the extra equipment Valentina had strapped to her back (an amazing feat in itself, considering the woman's lithe frame and tiny structure), she suited up the others. There was no doubt she had done this many times before. One after the other, the women rappelled down the ice wall. Dani followed Dr. Frankel, Valentina being the last.

The moment Valentina's feet touched the hard-packed snow, they heard the popping sound of gunfire. The battle had begun.

SCENE 37

THE FIGHT

The thought of impending death for many exploited staff both saddens and angers Dani.

Knowing some of the insiders were mere pawns in the hands of evil and powerful men made Dani angry. Very angry. Innocent lives would be lost today. The security guard she had injured, his name is Will Bradson. He has a name. Who knows if he wasn't another of Bacardi's pawns. *Enough of that. Focus. Let it go. You did what you had to do. Maybe he'll make it. Oh God, I pray he does.*

Dani scanned the terrain for Jack and Jason. She saw only a blanket of white with a background of blowing snow. Vaguely, she could see the terrain was made up of waves of snow mounds, which would help to protect them from incoming fire.

In the calm before the storm, Dani suddenly had a strange but comforting feeling. She sensed they were not alone. *Extraterrestrial beings? Waring Angels?*

"There, over there," Marcie yelled. "That flashing light." Dani snapped back to the task at hand. She saw it too, a light, flashing Morse code, dimmed in the haze, far in the distance. She read, got—your—back—Jack.

A wave of relief and excitement hit her. Jack was close. Should they live through this, the next few minutes would determine the rest of their lives. Everything suddenly seemed so surreal.

In seconds, Dani and the others stripped off their climbing gear, and with AR17's ready to fire, stealthily they made their way towards the intermittent flashing lights. This time Valentina took the lead. A few steps later, the firefight started, closer this time, and they were the targets.

Becky was the first casualty. With a sharp cry, she was lifted off her feet and flew forward several yards, landing hard on her stomach. Before anyone could reach her, a fast-moving, white object appeared out of nowhere.

Bentley? It didn't take Dani more than a mere second to recognize him, despite his camouflage. The black snout and stubby tail were tell-tale giveaways. Then, seeing Marcie and Becky had positioned their gun sites on Bentley, Dani blocked them and shouted, "No, don't shoot. That's Bentley. He'll take care of Becky and get her to safety." Dani scrambled over to Becky.

"I'm OK," Becky said, sounding just a little winded. Got me in the thigh is all."

"You'll be just fine, Becky. Trust Bentley. He knows what he's doing." Dani said as she turned to return fire. The shots were nearer and louder now.

By now, everyone focused on the incoming fire; the operatives, crouched near the ground, were answering fire with fire. As far as they were concerned, they had an advantage, a huge advantage. They were perfectly trained, and they reacted as they were trained. They were also resilient and not easy to eliminate. They were in their element. This was what they did best.

Bentley kept on task. He was so focused, Dani was glad he hadn't recognized her. Best to let him do his job. He grabbed hold of Becky's jacket, dug his ice-gripper doggy boots into the hard-packed snow and began dragging her behind a snowbank and towards the plane. Bentley, powerfully built, had jaws of steel. Becky, being not more than 120 lb., was an easy package for him to manage.

With gunfire also coming from Jack and his team, the place lit up like a New Year's eve celebration. *Kurt. Where is that man? What's that Dr. Frankel up to?*

Dani made a quick check and was relieved to see he was in fine shape. Dr. Frankel's right hand tightly clutched the pocket that contained his tiny precious vials. But with his other hand, he skillfully fired a UMP submachine gun. (Universal Machine Pistol) The second pocket was full of vials as well, but Dani was thankful to see the Dr. was willing to risk losing at least some of his irreplaceable supplies. *Well, we know that man's got what it takes. Surprise, surprise, he's not just a crazy scientist.*

Amid the firefight, the sounds of incoming aircraft filled the air. *They're here and right on time too—The Chief and Jack's buddies.* Dani could see the outline of the chopper. Before it landed, she saw several figures jump out the side door and begin opening fire non-stop into the advancing guards.

"Reinforcements!" Dani shouted. "Let's make a run for it," she yelled to her comrades. "They've got us covered. Let's go. Let's go. GO, GO, GO."

In quick response, the troop kept their heads down and ran towards the helicopter. Dr. Frankel stumbled. The Dr. was the second one to take a hit. From the corner of her eye, Gracie, closest to him, saw him stumble then fall to the ground gripping his mid-section. Without hesitation, Gracie stopped, turned and ran back to the injured man. Effortlessly she swooped him up into her arms, and in one smooth move, hardly missing a beat, she kept on running.

Bullets were flying everywhere. Ever-so-often, they heard a yell, letting them know one of the guards had taken a hit.

Considering all the bullets that flew past them that day, they made it without further incident to the Sea King—something they would later say was only but for the grace of God.

The doctor groaned as he clutched his gut, his jacket now drenched in red. Gracie gently planted him down on the ground and ripped open his clothing. Dani dropped down beside Gracie, and Dr. Gracie gave Dani the look that said, "this is bad." Gracie pressed her hands down hard on the wound to contain the bleeding.

In an instant, Dani made a decision. She would not be moved by what she saw. She would speak life to the situation. She felt it rise up inside of her; she heard herself say, "Dr. Frankel, I know you know the severity of your injuries. Nobody's kidding anybody; this is bad. But I'm saying this about that; you will live and not die. You listen to me, and you press down on that wound, and we'll get you through this."

Through gritted teeth, the Dr. replied. "I can do a lot of things to preserve the human body, and I am quite an impressive specimen of the human race, I know, (he took a breath and held it there for a second), and I've taken hits before," he went on, "but there's something different about this one. I'm not so sure my time isn't up. Thing is," he sucked in another breath of air; "I'm not ready to die. We've still got some talking to do, you and I—about important things—you know."

"I know. Listen, Kurt. I've said you are going to live. That's it. Now, just do as you're told!

"You hear that, Dr. Frankel. You do as she says," Gracie added. "You're gonna live."
\
"Yes, Ma'am." Dr. Frankel made a feeble attempt to salute.

Dani put her hand on the Dr.'s and whispered an urgent prayer. Her hand still on his, she assessed her surroundings.

Just then, Valentina dropped down next to the Dr. and Dani. "I've got this," she pulled a medic kit out of her bag. "This will stop the bleeding some. It's OK, I got EMT training."

"You are a woman of surprises," Dani said. "Kurt, you're in great hands."

"Gracie, you stay here and cover. Watch out for Bentley and Becky. They're bound to show up soon. Nobody gets near this helicopter, you hear."

"Copy that. Nobody's gonna get past me or die on my watch."

"I don't doubt that for a moment," Dani replied while once again she triple-checked their surroundings. Dani noted Marcie, Kelly and Sandra. She counted seven other friendlies. Those would be Jack's buddies; who was who, she couldn't tell. Chief Lance, Clay, Mack, Billy, Pete, Cam and J.D.

But where is Jack? Then she spotted him. That had to be him. It was him! Shivers rippled through her body. Hope and confidence soared. The impossible is happening.

Another man, smaller in stature, crouched next to Jack. *Is that Jason? That is Jason Whiting! Mr. Starbucks, boy, you surprise me. One never really knows what you're capable of until you get pushed off the cliff. Jason, you are something else. Look at you handle that weapon like a pro. Jack taught you how to do that. I'll bet on it.*

The next moment, as expected, Bentley arrived, still pulling Becky by her parka hood. Becky. Looking backward with Uzi in hand, relentlessly fired shots at the approaching guards. She appeared to be in good shape.

Bentley released her when he got to the side of the open helicopter doors. Dani couldn't have been more thankful and more proud of Bentley than she was at that moment. For such a time as this. Retired and still saving lives.

"Hold your fire for just a second, OK, Becky." Dani dropped next to Becky to assess her wound. The bleeding had slowed down considerably, probably due to the cold more than shock. Dani could see Becky was in fine, firing spirits. "Becky, you show me up, girl. We'll be out of here in no time."

"You can bet on that," Becky answered. "No bullsh**-bullet's gonna do me in that easy."

Dani turned to Bentley. "Bentley, you incredible dog. I love you."

Bentley had been watching her intently. When she called his name, he cocked his head to the side, a quizzical look on his beautiful, handsome face. Then he yelped and jumped into her arms, whining a greeting of absolute delight. Of course, he recognized her. Bentley would always recognize her regardless of what she looked or smelled like.

With no time to waste, Dani pulled out the ripped pocket belonging to the Major. "Bentley, track and rescue," she gave the command. "Bentley whined and sniffed the cloth. (Track and rescue meant friendly, track and subdue meant enemy.)

Knowing what to do, with a quick swipe of his tongue across Dani's face, Bentley gave one more delighted yelp before racing off towards the action. He was all business and back to the task at hand. Fearlessly the battle-worn K9 ran into the firefight and disappeared into the darkness.

Dani snapped to attention and pulled herself together. *If the Major is out there and still alive, Bentley will bring him home.*

"Let's get this over with," she muttered as she ran towards Jack. Dani planted herself next to him. Neither took the time to acknowledge the other; each kept their focus on the enemy mere meters away. Jack never missed a beat, but he knew—he could feel her; he did not have to look at the figure next to him to know it was his beloved Dani. He did not need to see her scar nor did he need to hear the code word. He could feel her.

SCENE 38

OUT OF HERE-ALMOST

The shooting has stopped. A whistling wind accompanies the eerie silence. In the distance, someone moans and breaks the silence. A few seconds later, a snarl, followed by a yell.

***

"Hold your fire." Chief Copper yelled, "Not sure what's going on out there, but I think we've done some damage. It sounds like Bentley's taking care of a few loose ends."

"Bentley's got this," Jack said.

The Chief nodded. "He is one of our best assets. He knows how to sneak up on the enemy like any good Navy Seal."

The Chief turned and shouted the order. "Time to move! We're getting out of here! Everybody, to the helo! Now!".

"Wait," Dani said. "We're missing one of ours," Sergeant Major Madson, our trainer. I've sent Bentley to find him."

"We can't leave without Sergeant Major," both Marcy and Sandra stated in unison, having walked within range of the conversation.

"He stayed behind to do as much damage as possible from the inside," Dani added. "No one would have suspected him of being one of us. He said he'd meet up with us. My gut says he's out there somewhere, alive."

"We won't leave anyone behind," Jack assured them.

Then Jack and Dani locked eyes. "Can the phone," she said slyly. Jack smiled.

"I knew it was you," he said. "Love you," he mouthed. And she mouthed "Love you" back.

"Is that Dani?" Jason asked.

"That's Dani," Jack answered.

"Wow! How'd you know?"

"Pay attention, Jason. I just know. Now focus. We can all get acquainted when this is over and we are safe.

"Right. OK. But what about my dad's plane?" Jason continued as they ran towards the aircraft. "We can't leave his plane out here. He'll have my hide."

"Jason, we'll come back for it when it's safe. I think your dad will understand. He'd rather have you than the plane," Jack answered.

"We'll come back for it then," Jason agreed.

The Chief and Mack stood watch, UMPs poised. As Marcie swooped Becky up in her arms and nimbly jumped into the chopper. Sandra did the same with the doc. In less than a minute, everyone was on the helicopter; everyone except for Bentley and the Sergeant Major. Jack whistled. They waited. Every second was like a lifetime.

Another 30 seconds passed. The engines were running and ready for takeoff.

"We're not leaving without them," Dani stated. "We've agreed to that and that's the Navy Seal way."

"You bet we're not. Not a chance," Becky responded.

"How do you want to handle this?" the Chief asked Jack.

"We don't have any more time to waste." Jack jumped out of the plane. This ship has to get into the air now if any of us want to live to see another day."

Jack addressed the Chief, Clay, Mack, Billy, Pete. "I'll stay behind, besides the Sargent Major, Bentley and myself. Jason's Beechcraft's got room for one more person. Before he could finish, all five of his former Navy Seal comrades moved to join him.

Dani gave a short gasp and stood to her feet, pushing the men aside. Before she could say anything, Jason announced, "I'm hangin' in with you." He jumped out and took a determined stance in front of Jack. It's my plane we're gonna need to get us out of here, and I'm not leaving without it," he said bravely.

"Jason, you get back in that chopper."

"No, Sir, I'm the pilot!"

"Jason, that's an order. Get back in that helo. You've risked your life enough for one day," Jack said, more kindly this time.

"Yes, Sir." Reluctantly, Jason climbed back into the plane and settled in between Sandra and Valentina. Valentina slipped her hand into Jason's, and the tension drained from his face. One could even see a slight smile creep across his face if one was paying attention.

Dani came over to Jack and the group. "Dr. Frankel says to expect a drone to arrive any minute now."

"A drone you say. We better move it then." Briefly, Jack addressed the men. They agreed Jack and the Chief would stay behind.

"Now, everybody out of here. That's an order," the Chief stated. "Your job is to get everyone including this helo to Aklavik in one piece."

"I'm staying with you, Jack," Dani said, ready to disembark. *I do not want to spend another hour separated from you, Jack.*

"That's not going to work," Jack replied, a gentleness in his voice. "Jason's Beechcraft only has four seats, Dani. It'll be OK. I'll see you in Aklavik before you know it. It's only about 20 minutes away. We didn't get this far just on our own. God's not going to fail us now."

Dani's confidence settled in. "No, he won't," she answered. Psalm 91 began playing in her mind. Known as the soldier's Psalm, Dani was very familiar with the passage. For many years, millions of soldiers have carried this Psalm with them into battle, written on a card or dog tag, or bandana. *He who dwells in the secret place of the most High, will abide under the shadow of the Almighty.* Dani settled into her seat and fastened her seatbelt. *I will say of the Lord, He is my refuge and my fortress, my God in whom I trust….* At that moment, Dani knew that she knew that she knew everything would be OK. *…He will give His angels charge over you, to guard you in all of your ways….* She had felt their presence, and even now, she sensed they were near.

"I'll be seeing you soon, Dani. That's a promise." Jack reached in and grabbed his Dani's hand, looking intensely into her beautiful eyes. She felt his strength, his confidence.

"You better," Dani replied. "Now, go."

Jack withdrew his hand and closed the door of the chopper.

Unexpectedly, Dani's eyes began to tear up. Quickly she wiped them dry with her sleeve and sucked in a deep breath. She hadn't cried for a very long time. She was surprised at the emotions welling up inside of her. She felt human again, just knowing she could still cry. But crying would have to wait.

Jack and the Chief grew smaller and smaller as the helo lifted into the air. Everyone was well aware that their situation was still dire. Some assassins could still be waiting to fire missiles.

Several minutes would pass before takeoff was considered "uneventful." Sighs of relief filled the Sea King as it flew into the thick clouds.

SCENE 39

LEFT BEHIND?

Based on training and past experiences, Jack and the Chief agree that, most likely, Bentley and the Sergeant, if still alive, have found safety and are well out of range of the facility by now. They are confident in Bentley's training to feel vibrations, to understand their significance and know how to react. Also, Bentley, as is with all dogs, can hear sounds many times stronger than humans, as well as a wider range of sounds and frequencies, sounds humans cannot detect.

Jack and the Chief had almost reached the Beechcraft when in unison, the two men stopped dead in their tracks. "It's coming," the Chief said.

The Chief and Jack dropped to the snow-covered ground and lay prostrate, blending in as one with the landscape, listening for the drone. They waited—they heard it.

Fire lit up the sky, and a cloud of smoke and debris from the Spy or Die facility flew into the air. The men stayed put, expecting a second blast. Sure enough, the drone made a wide circle and dropped another bomb for good measure.

Once the smoke had somewhat settled, and they deemed it safe, Jack and the Chief set to work. Every few minutes, Jack whistled, hoping to hear Bentley's bark in response. Frequently, the men stopped to reassess their surroundings, checking bodies scattered about the terrain, looking for the Major. It was a messy sight that brought back difficult and even terrifying memories of previous battles. Their resolve to complete their mission kept them going and kept their heads on straight.

Then they heard him, Bentley's welcomed barks coming from the direction of the Beechcraft.

"Bentley's made his way back to ground zero," Jack said, relief in his voice.

"Sounds like he's OK," the Chief responded. "Let's meet up with him and then we can circle the area, see if we can locate the Sergeant.

"He's staying put," Jack said. "That's his tell bark. I think he's got his man, and we need to get to them ASAP."

The men picked up their pace.

SCENE 40

IT'S A WRAP

When Jack and the Chief get to the Beechcraft, they find a panting Bentley laying down next to the Major, who is sitting, legs stretched out in front of him, back leaning against the aircraft wheel. Bentley sees Jack and whines a greeting, then puts his head on the Major's knee, indicating all is well. His eyes and eyebrows communicate all that is needed. The Major acknowledges the men's presence, then looks down at Bentley and puts his arm around the dog's back, showing his gratitude. Both appear exhausted. The Major's now bloodstained headpiece is wrapped around his right forearm.

"Sergeant Major, it looks like you and K9 Bentley found each other. I'm Seattle Police Chief Lance Copper, and this is Ex-Navy Seal, Jack Wells." The Major had started to get up. "As is, Major."

"Thank you, Sirs. I am more than grateful to see you. I'm just a little spent but be assure my recovery rate is exemplary. We had a dozen targets on our backs we needed to take down, Bentley and I, and we took a little damage."

"We're just glad to see you are all in one piece."

"So am I. Sir, this has been the worst day of my life and the best day of my life. I never thought I would get free of those tyrants. I never thought I'd live past today, 'cept for this incredible dog here, and your Jane Russel or Dani, as you know her. I owe my life to the both of them. This incredible super dog here! I can't even describe it. He is supernaturally fast and deadly accurate. Our targets never knew what hit them. They didn't have time to react. He was so fast, went straight for the jugular, and as I said, I have never seen anything like it."

"Bentley is quite the miracle dog. And he has a habit of doing that. Saving people, that is, don't you, Bentley?" Jack sat down next to his dog and the Major. "We do have a lot to be thankful for today."

Gently Jack removed Bentley's blood-stained and ripped battle-scarred gear. He ran his hands over the dog, checking for injuries. He found a nasty 3 inch cut under his chin, which would need stitches, a torn ear, and the area around his old wound was tender. Jack determined none of the injuries were life-threatening but would need some tender loving care.

"You're going to be OK, Bentley boy. We'll get you home and all fixed up, good as new." The exhausted Bentley licked Jack's face and nestled his head into his master's chest. Lovingly, Jack wrapped his arms around his buddy and breathed a deep sigh of relief.

"We've got one more thing to attend to," the Major said. "I was able to secure six staff in the Safety Chamber, all of whom are unwilling participants in this project. Since the chamber is built to withstand the most deadly of blasts, I trust they are still alive. The chamber is fully supplied for several weeks. Following Dr. Frankel's safety profile, we need to wait forty-eight hours before entering the chamber. The entry code is 007 288 247."

"Survivors? That is very good news!" Jack responded. "007 288 247."

"Awesome! Nice work, Sargeant Major. We'll notify the authorities once in Aklavik," the Chief said. "I gotta say, this has been one mind-blowing experience. I think I'm going to need some serious debriefing."

"You are not alone," Jack responded. "Know, I'm there for you, any time you want to talk."

"I think I'll take you up on that."

"It's a wrap, then. Let's get out of here. I have some serious catching up to do with Dani." A smile crossed Jack's face.

Bentley gave a sharp bark at the mention of Dani's name. " And Bentley and I, we could use a juicy, 12 oz. Angus beef steak and a few hours of solid sleep. What' yah say to that, Buddy."

Bentley gave an enthusiastic howl.

"Copy that!" the Major and Chief said in unison.

SCENE 41

THE INCREDIBLE EVER AFTER
ONE YEAR LATER

**The Rescue & Restore
Mission Statement:**
*To relentlessly fight on behalf of all
women and children, against domestic
violence and human trafficking, to set
them free from the hands of their
abusers, and to be an instrument of
hope and change.*

**Dani on assignment
undercover**

Within a very short time, **Operation
Rescue and Restore** had become well-
known in the underground "Fight for
Freedom" movement, a movement gaining momentum in many parts
of the world.

The Rescue and Restore team consists of Jack, K9 Bentley, Clay,
Mack, Billy and Pete, Sergeant Major Madson, and Dani and her
Spy or Die project comrades, Kelly, Becky, Marcie, Sandra and
Gracie.

Their lives forever changed, they have given themselves to fighting
evildoers and saving and protecting the innocent, abused and exploited.

On assignment, this highly trained team is heavily armed, extremely dangerous to the enemy and effective. Skilled in both espionage and undercover work, the formidable team boldly and relentlessly pursues their target. They always get their "man."

And what about Dr. Frankel? Dr. Frankel finally found his true passion. Miraculously, he has come to peace with not living forever on planet Earth. Having encountered the God of the universe in a very personal way, he now knows his future in the after life is going to be more than **HE** could ever design or imagine. The Dr. has never been happier or more content.

At the Rescue and Restore compound, Dr. Frankel is Director of Research. He is also Head of Surgery and the medical decision-maker at their twenty-four-bed, recently constructed hospital. Needless to say, under Dr. Frankel's supervision, the facility is state-of-the-art and beyond. Anyone entering the premises is subjected to tight security measures and is vigorously screened and monitored.

Along with a team of dedicated-to-the-cause medical staff, the facility is equipped to handle everything from minor injuries to amputations and reconstructive procedures. The Rescue and Restore hospital is financed by like-minded, silent partners from all over the world.

As Chaplain, the kind and wise Rev. Graham provides the weary and battered souls with spiritual guidance and life-skills counselling. Healing the soul is a number one priority at Rescue and Restore.

Situated on a glassy, underground spring-fed lake on some twenty acres. (again a donation by silent partners) Rescue and Restore has completed the following: Twelve fully furnished cabins, a rehab facility, a meeting and dining lodge, an outdoor training arena, a lunch bar, coffee shop and library combined. A sports/aqua indoor training facility is under construction.

A thriving vegetable and flower garden is nestled near the lake.

Both garden therapy and animal therapy are an integral part of Rescue and Restore.

An endearing Newfoundland dog, Athena, takes her therapy job very seriously and is loved by everyone she meets. Bentley and Athena are best of friends.

The nearly untouched wilderness of flora and fauna is the perfect place for exhilarating and adventurous training excursions.

On rescue missions, the team comprises those on the frontlines, those who take care of the incoming rescued at the rescue site base, and those who stay back to hold the fort.

Many of the rescued women and children are so traumatized from enduring sexual abuse and often debilitating torture; they need immediate attention. Loving care is administered freely. Those with life-threatening injuries are choppered out to the nearest medical facility.

Jason and Valentina? They are madly in love. With Jack's help, as he promised, Valentina is now a legal citizen of the United States.

She is a valued part of the physical training program for the women's arm of the Adventure in Attitudes Boot Camp. Jason is continuing with his studies and will soon see his dream of becoming a Forensic Science Technician come true.

The Chief, true to his promise, organized a neighborhood police watch on Union Street.

One of the officers with soccer skills took on coaching the side-street team every Saturday morning. Little Jimmy's mother, Heather, thinks besides being fun to be around, this officer is pretty darn good-looking. But she's keeping that to herself, for now.

Does this all sound like one happy ending? This is not the end.

Considering the life choice these warriors have chosen, one can only imagine the challenges and dangers they are bound to encounter.

No, not all times will be happy times, but the satisfaction they get from silencing monsters and setting the innocent free is happiness, and a deep sense of fulfillment..

SCENE 42

IN PEACE WILL I LIE DOWN & SLEEP

Presently, the Rescue and Restore team is tracking twenty-seven dangerous offenders. The location where six of the perpetrators are in hiding has recently been identified. The Rescue and Restore team takes to the air at 0 6:15 hours, with the intent to capture and arrest said six dangerous offenders within seventy-two hours.

The night before deployment.

Sitting in front of a warm, cozy fire in their living room, Jack and Dani are enjoying each other's company while sipping on hot Hazelnut decaf Latte'. Bentley is sprawled at their feet.

Dani gave a big sigh and sinks deep into the cozy couch. "Tomorrow's another big day. Here we are, about to take on our sixth mission in several months."

"You are amazing, Dani. Who would have thought so much good would come out of the terrible situation you were caught up in just months ago."

"Everyone's been amazing. And we've just got started."

"I can't understate. This mission is a highly dangerous one. More so than the others. We are going to infiltrate terrorist hideouts, and we could have casualties. It's time-sensitive and requires precise execution. I know, I know. We've gone over this relentlessly."

"Jack, we can never be too prepared."

"So, you are ready for tomorrow then?" Jack looked at Dani, curled up beside him. Reaching over, he touched the scar on Dani's cheek. She did not flinch.

"I'm ready. And you?" Dani asked.

"More than ready."

"Well, I say that about wraps it up. What about you, Bentley, you got all that? Course you do. What would we do without you, you big, loveable superdog?" Dani placed a hand on the dozing dog lying at their feet.

Bentley yawned, sat up and stretched. Then nimbly jumped on the couch next to Dani and laid his head on her lap.

"You're right, Bentley," Jack said. Enough for today. Let tomorrow take care of itself. I'm going to bed, and I'm going to sleep like a Bentley."

"Copy that."

> ***"In peace will I both lie down and sleep,***
> ***for it is God alone who makes me to dwell in safety."***
> ***(Psalm 4:8)***

NARRATION

Somewhere out there, right now, real-life true warriors are risking their lives to rescue captives from the clutches of human trafficking monsters. Plans made in secret and implemented at the dead of night are taking place as I write.

The physical and spiritual battle against such evildoers is not for the faint of heart. We know this gets messy. The rescuers are subjected to the elements and unknown dangers. People get injured. Some die, often violently.

But, the rescued get a chance to live again, be cared for and feel loved.

I've been following the activities of a certain man and his wife on social media. They are a couple who have a unshakable belief in God and the teachings of the Bible. Here is where I gleaned good information for the human trafficking element of my story.

A former Marine, the man is a "high-risk humanitarian." He and his wife are both skilled in military-based self-defence. This skill has opened the door for educating and training others in self-protection and human trafficking awareness.

He is officially known as "the world's fastest gun disarm man."

It takes him .08 seconds.

He has a seventh-degree black belt in Keichu-do karate and jiu-jitsu and a fourth-degree black belt-in weapons. Mrs. holds a second-degree black belt.

Along with a team of like-minded and trained experts, this couple regularly participates in well-planned and executed rescue missions, ones that at times take them into extremely dangerous parts of the world. And, they do get their "man."

There's so much more to this couple than I've shared. You might want to do some searching for yourself and see what they and are up to.

Carrie Wachsmann

THE SOLDIER'S PSALM
PSALM 91

He who dwells in the shelter of the Most High
Will abide in the shadow of the Almighty.
I will say to the Lord, "My refuge and my fortress,
My God, in whom I trust!"
For it is He who delivers you from the snare of the trapper
And from the deadly pestilence.
He will cover you with His pinions,
And under His wings you may seek refuge;
His faithfulness is a shield and bulwark.

You will not be afraid of the terror by night,
Or of the arrow that flies by day;
Of the pestilence that stalks in darkness,
Or of the destruction that lays waste at noon.
A thousand may fall at your side
And ten thousand at your right hand,
But it shall not approach you.
You will only look on with your eyes
And see the recompense of the wicked.
For you have made the Lord, my refuge,
Even the Most High, your dwelling place.
No evil will befall you,
Nor will any plague come near your tent.

For He will give His angels charge concerning you,
To guard you in all your ways.
They will bear you up in their hands,
That you do not strike your foot against a stone.
You will tread upon the lion and cobra,
The young lion and the serpent you will trample down.

"Because he has loved Me, therefore I will deliver him;
I will set him securely on high, because he has known My name.
"He will call upon Me, and I will answer him;
I will be with him in trouble;
I will rescue him and honor him.
"With a long life I will satisfy him
And let him see My salvation."

Carrie's BLOG: carriewachsmann.com/blog2

ABOUT THE AUTHOR

Carrie's interest in the arts began as a young girl. An imaginative child, she loved to draw, read, write and listen to stories. Their three room school library consisted of a mere three short shelves of books, not nearly enough to satisfy her need for creative reading and storytelling.

After school, Carrie would often run home to sit down beside their old fashioned, console radio and listen to Aunt Ollie—a half hour program where Aunt Ollie read fables, mysteries, and other delightful tales.

Carrie's passion for storytelling and desire to create continued after marriage and children. She took several writing courses as well as pursuing painting, drawing and film making.

She writes for both adults and children, fantasy and adventure being her favorite.

Carrie has a M.Ministry (Professional Writer) and D.Ministry (Fine Arts and Media).

Awards: Outstanding Emerging Artist - Arty Award
                Outstanding Literary Artist - Arty Award

Author's website: http://www.carriewachsmann.com/blog2

The Ryder- A Fantasy Adventure
Treasure Trap, a sequel to ***The Ryder***
Newfies to the Rescue- Tales of the Newfoundland Dog
Roadblocks to Hell, A Story of Redemption
http://roadblockstohell.com
Chuzzle's Incredible Journey, co-authored (daughter)
Finding Christmas - A Mouse in Search of Christmas
KickStart to a Healthier You

Published by

HeartBeat Productions Inc.
Box 633
Abbotsford, BC, Canada V2T 6Z8
email: **info@heartbeat1.com**
website: **heartbeat1.com**
604.852.3761

Made in the USA
Middletown, DE
14 November 2021